MIDNIGHT Macarons

FLEUR DEVILLAINY

 Formatted with Vellum

TRIGGER WARNING

Midnight Macarons is a work of adult paranormal romance and not intended for minors. It contains scenes that may be distressing to some people including strong language, violence, cheating, drinking and sexual content.

For those who give too much, feel too deep, love too hard and don't expect anything in return.

CHAPTER 1
ROSE

You can do this. It's just a present.

That's what I keep telling myself, but the words taste sour in my mouth.

The little bell over the art supply shop door chimes as I step inside, the familiar scent of turpentine and paper tugging at old memories.

I inhale slowly, then exhale even slower.

It's quiet. Still. The kind of still that makes you feel like the air is listening. The kind of silence that makes the thoughts in your head overly obtrusive.

I can't let that deter me. Not the silence. Not the crippling anxiety whispering that I might be making the wrong choice.

"Hello?" My voice breaks the hush, more to drown out my own thoughts than to summon anyone. I glance down each aisle, scanning the signs at the top of the shelves—acrylic paint, canvas—until I land on the one I'm looking for: paintbrushes and tools.

"Bingo," I whisper, forcing nonchalance while every instinct in me screams that this could be a mistake. Pretend it's just a normal trip, a normal girlfriend buying her boyfriend a normal anniversary gift.

But it's not.

I've been here plenty of times with him, watching as he compared brushes, picked apart pigments, told stories about colors like they were old friends. But this time is different. This time I'm not trailing behind him on an errand after a long day.

This time, I'm here for our anniversary.

One year.

The longest I've ever stayed. The longest I've ever let myself stay without cutting ties and running, afraid of being tethered to someone.

And for the first time, I want to give him something real. Something that says I might be staying for good.

I run my fingers along the smooth wooden handles, the bristles protected in tiny plastic sleeves. I don't know much about art, but after eleven months of silent observation, I've learned enough. His emotions have always been easy for me to read—too easy. Even without calling on my magic. Not that I try. Everyone deserves their privacy, but when he's constantly blasting feelings like a stereo cranked to eleven, it's impossible not to notice.

And every time we stopped here, he always beelined for this aisle, pausing in front of one particular item.

A set of sable-hair brushes.

The kind that will cost me nearly a month's rent. But this is our one-year anniversary—the longest I've ever been with anyone—and tonight I want everything to be perfect. Including the gift.

So why does nausea churn in my gut as I press the little red button for help beside the glass case?

"Just pre-event jitters," I mutter, waiting as the elderly shopkeeper hobbles out from the back.

Twenty minutes later, I pull into an empty parking spot behind the club. My gaze flicks to the neatly wrapped package on the passenger seat: a gift for Jett. The brushes he's been eyeing for months, out of his budget as a budding artist. Out of mine too, if I hadn't been picking up extra gigs. Still, it's small compared to the rest of tonight.

For months, I've been orchestrating this day—securing The Rubbish Toads, his favorite rock band, to play a show in the suburbs of Greyhaven. It took every favor I could call in: connections from my college internships and the triplet fae sisters who own the exclusive Summerwind club. Landing them a performance slot wasn't easy. Since starting my job at the event center, I've been working with the sisters to book clients for private parties and events at their club, and that relationship finally paid off.

It's been a lot. But all of it builds to this night, our one-year anniversary.

And tonight, I'm going to ask Jett to move in with me.

He hasn't *officially*, but he's practically lived with me between various art jobs, spending more nights at my place than his own.

I'm afraid of commitment. Afraid of letting someone connect to me so deeply. That's why I always cut ties before things get serious. Not that I'd ever cared enough to want to take them further.

Well—except once. One guy. One wolf, for that matter.

In a single weekend—no, in a single kiss—he made my magic hum, made me feel alive in ways I still can't explain. So much that I ran. I was too afraid to face my own feelings, too afraid to risk what it might mean: the chance to be free, to explore the world, to chase my passions.

We're not even going to go there. That was the past, and I've moved on. Even if his blue eyes still haunt my dreams. I wasn't ready to commit back then. But I am now.

I think.

"You deserve this, Rose. You give so much—you deserve love and happiness," I murmur as I grab my black leather purse. Its cool, smooth exterior steadies my clammy palm as I fumble with my jangling keys. I head for the backstage door, willing my nerves away.

I glance at my watch, the numbers sharp against the pale face. Two hours until showtime. I told Jett to meet me here an hour before the band goes on, promising him a backstage tour and a chance to meet them. I meant to keep it a surprise, but I'm terrible at surprises and slipped about who was playing. What I didn't tell him was everything it took to get them here —and that I did it all for him.

Jett and I met over a year ago, right after I came back from visiting my best friend, Netti. I was searching for something— freedom, expression, adventure—I wasn't sure. What I did know was that I wasn't ready to settle down. After too many years under my parents' thumb, stifled by their expectations, I wanted more than the neat little path laid out for me.

I love my small town, with its mix of witches and supernatural beings, but I craved something beyond it. Like most witches, I can manage the basics: levitating objects, weaving enchantments, brewing potions that sparkle with charm. But I also have something rarer, an ability that thrives on connecting with and helping others—an empathy magic that feeds on shared emotions.

That's what pulled me into event planning. It's demanding, yes, but it gives me freedom—the chance to travel and bring joy to people's lives. And that's why I fell so hard for Jett. He sees the vibrant energy in me, encourages me to chase my dreams. As a fellow artist, he understands my need for creative expression and growth, mirroring my own aspirations.

Yesterday I'd checked in with The Rubbish Toads, made sure their equipment arrived, oversaw soundcheck, smoothed every detail. The triplet fae sisters assured me this would be a roaring success.

Still, a nervous energy prickles under my skin as the key slides into the lock. The muffled thrum of tuning guitars and low, vibrating drums hums through the air, and a smile tugs at my lips. Then the knot of anxiety twists in my stomach again.

Why am I so anxious?

"You've got this, Rose," I whisper, pepping myself up for the third time today as I weave through stacks of equipment and boxes.

The dark backstage wraps around me like a balm, familiar with its musty odor of old instruments, the metallic tang of strings, the faint bite of cleaner. Here I'm in my element: coordinating the chaos, making sure everything runs smoothly, ensuring tonight is perfect.

A high-pitched squeal shatters the moment, followed by heavy breathing and muffled moans. I pinch the bridge of my nose, exasperated. I don't have time for amorous teenagers—or worse, a groupie tangled up with a band member. Whatever they do on their own time is fine, but right now I have a job: get everything ready before Jett arrives so we can enjoy the evening together.

Besides, I have kissing of my own planned.

Rounding another stack of boxes, I freeze. In the dim

lighting of the backstage, I make out a man with long bleached hair and pale skin, pants around his ankles, pounding into a blonde sprawled across a pile of instrument cases. Her dress is bunched at her waist, hair splayed, breasts bouncing with every thrust. Heat floods my face as I slap a hand over my eyes, but the image is already seared into my mind.

"I don't know who you are, but this is not the time or place. You have two minutes to make yourselves presentable and leave before I call security," I say sharply, turning away and tapping my foot against the wooden floor.

"Rose?"

My stomach plummets at the familiar voice, a chill racing down my spine.

The man who isn't supposed to be here for another hour.

Jett.

CHAPTER 2
ROSE

I groan as I pull on slacks and button up my shirt, bracing for another day at work. The buttercream-yellow blouse patterned with white daisies—usually my favorite—stares back at me in the mirror. Yellow is supposed to be a happy color, a symbol of positivity and light.

At least, it used to be.

"One foot in front of the other, Rose. You're a strong, powerful witch. You don't need some man to define you," I tell my reflection, studying the sallow tint of my cheeks. I pinch the skin, paste on a smile.

If only it were that easy.

Grabbing my toothbrush, I squeeze out a glob of pink shimmer-berry toothpaste and attack the invisible plaque with a vengeance that would make the tooth fairy proud. But even my favorite kid-flavored toothpaste tastes like ash.

When did I go from party girl—happy-go-lucky, ready to take on the world—to this wreck?

Since the night you found your boyfriend, on your anniversary, fucking some blonde bimbo.

My fists clench around the sink. The light bulbs flicker with the surge of my magic.

Pull it together, Rose. He's not worth it.

My phone buzzes against the porcelain, my heart stuttering, but I ignore it. Instead, I twist my long auburn hair into a business ponytail, slicking down flyaways with a dab of pomade. With summer's heat creeping in, I'll never fully tame the waves, but spring's chill gives me a fighting chance. I finish with SPF moisturizer and a touch of mascara. Simple but efficient.

Fake it until you make it. Right?

The phone buzzes again. Twice. My jaw tightens. Maybe it's not him. Maybe it's Netti, or my parents, or a delivery notification, I tell myself as I flip it over. Hell, I'd settle for spam.

Jett: Hey, Babe.

Buzz.

Jett: Please text me back.

Buzz.

Jett: Babe, it's been over a week. Are you done ignoring me?

Nope. I delete the messages and flip the phone over, nausea churning in my stomach.

I should block him. But every time I try, guilt needles me. People make mistakes, right?

I just wasn't ready to forgive him. *If ever.*

Netti had warned me long before that night to kick him to the curb. She never liked him. I thought she just didn't *get* him like I did.

Now I wonder if I ever did.

I push the thoughts aside. He isn't worth any more of my time—mental or otherwise. I have a good job, my own house—

Barking erupts outside, followed by a yowl.

What the hell?

I snatch the broom by the front door and rush outside, the irony of a witch with a broom not lost on me. I might not be able to fly away, but it's still a decent weapon—for intruders or ex-boyfriends.

The cold spring concrete bites at my bare feet as I creep across the crisp grass, broom clenched in my fist. But nothing waits at the side of the house, only tall old trees with fresh green leaves unfurling, buds tight at their roots.

"Maybe they ran off. I don't have time for this." I turn back toward the front door when a soft meow halts me.

Peering down, I spot a fluffy orange ball, no bigger than a grapefruit, poking its head out from under a bush against the house.

"Well, hello there, little one. Where did you come from?"

I scoop the orange tabby into my arms. Wide blue eyes blink up at me, pink-padded paws dangling, tiny body squirming. Definitely a boy.

"Easy there, mister. We don't want you falling."

I tuck him into my chest, scanning for his mother. His purr vibrates against me, sparking my magic to life.

"You're so tiny. Nothing but skin, bones, and fluff. Where's your family?" I whisper against his soft head, but there's no one around that I can see or sense.

Inside, I pour him a bowl of milk, which he greedily laps up before curling against my ankles.

"I can't keep you. I've got too much going on to take care of another creature. We'll find your family. What's your name?"

As if he'll answer, I lift him, fingers brushing over his soft stripes in search of a collar or tag to identify him. Nothing.

Perhaps he's chipped? I could take him to the shelter tomorrow if I left lunch early to check.

He purrs and nuzzles my palm, licking my thumb with his sandpaper tongue. Warmth floods me. I've been lonely since Jett—

Don't. Don't go there, Rose. Don't name the cat. You can't rescue every stray. Even if he is fluffy and warm and feels like home.

My phone buzzes again, and I toss it into my purse without looking. Can't he take a hint?

"Okay, kitty. I have to go to work, but tonight we'll post flyers. Tomorrow we'll check for a chip."

He meows, then hisses at my buzzing purse.

"Good boy," I murmur, stroking his head.

Maybe keeping him wouldn't be so bad if no one claims him. Every good witch needs a familiar, right?

"Fine." I crouch beside him, tapping my chin. "Tiger? Honey? Max?"

He stares at me as if saying, *really lady?*

I reach out to pet him, and he nips my finger.

"Hey there, Gingersnap—" He starts purring and licks the offended digit. "Ginger? You like that? You are quite spicy."

I chuckle as he nuzzles his head against the back of my hand.

"Ginger it is, at least until we find your family." I pat his head, and with my spirits lifted, I head to work.

THE DRIVE TO work is a blur, as is the rest of the morning.

A yawn slips out as I stretch before slumping back into my chair. Work at the event hall keeps me busy—busier than I'd like—but even the chaos can't quiet the part of me that dreads going home. The stillness waits there, heavy and hollow. I need... something else. Something I can't quite name.

My hand drifts to my chest, rubbing at the dull ache that never really leaves. It's been there for over a year now—a constant tug, like an invisible thread pulling taut from somewhere I can't see. Doctors ran tests and shrugged it off, chalking it up to anxiety and stress. And yes, I carry plenty of both—running the event hall full-time, living alone in a town far from family and old friends. But this feels different. Deeper.

I even turned to the magical community for answers. Netti —my best friend and one of the most talented potion witches I know—threw everything she had at the problem. Potions that fizzed and sparked, teas, charms, even her infamous enchanted baked goods. Dozens of remedies, and not one of them touched the ache.

Because it isn't just pain. It's grief without a name. Longing without a reason. Loss without ever having lost. And still, life presses forward. I have my work. I have my cat. I have enough. Or at least... I should.

If only my magic worked on me the way it does on others. Maybe then I could magic away this ache, even for a moment.

My phone buzzes. Anxiety hits like a wave, my body locking up. I thought I'd set it to Do Not Disturb so I could focus. What turned it off?

If he found a way to bypass—

I turn over the phone and stare at the caller ID. My chest constricts, breath stolen, heart hammering wildly as my palms grow clammy with sweat.

Angelique DeThistle. *The* Angelique DeThistle. Renowned owner of the Opal Pearl Lounge on the East Coast. I'd worked with her once, as an understudy during an internship project, and I'd sell my left kidney for the chance to work with her again.

"Rosemary Sinclaire speaking," I answer, praying I sound calmer than I feel.

"Ah, Rosemary." Angelique's French accent pours over the line. "I was hoping to reach you. I have a proposition."

"Of course. How can I help you?" I spin in my chair, yanking a notepad and pen from the desk drawer.

A million thoughts crowd my head, each one louder than the last. But the sharpest of them all—why is Angelique DeThistle calling me?

"After the project you worked on with me last year, I *knew* I needed to reach out when I heard you had relocated to Greyhaven."

I nearly knock over my coffee as her words sink in. I'd heard rumors she was planning to open a lounge for supernaturals on the West Coast. What I hadn't heard was *where*.

My phone buzzes with a text notification, rattling against my cheek. I grit my teeth. I only need one guess who that is. When will he stop?

"Rose? Are you still there?"

"Sorry, yes." I tap the pen against my temple, struggling to focus on her words instead of the flood of unwanted memories.

"Well," Angelique continues, "I've acquired a location in Greyhaven where I'd like to open a new lounge for supernaturals, and I'd love your help."

"A lounge here? In Greyhaven?" I echo, her words spinning through my head. Right in the backyard of the event hall I already manage.

"Yes. The contractors will be finished with the remodel in less than a month, but I'd love your feedback on the final touches. And, of course, I'd like you to run the grand opening night."

My stomach plummets. She wants me not just to weigh in on the remodel—she wants me to run the entire grand opening?

"I'd be honored," I reply, hoping I don't sound as breathless as I feel. *The* Angelique DeThistle wants me. She wants *me*. All those extra hours finally paying off. This could be the perfect opportunity for my resume.

And the perfect distraction I need.

Except... I already have a full-time job. Running a grand opening for a lounge to rival the Opal Pearl would take every free second I have—and then some.

"Fabulous. Meet me at seven tonight? It's on the corner of Thirteenth Street and Pathos. We can go over the details."

"That would be—wait, tonight?" I glance at my to-do list, then picture the kitten I left unsupervised, no doubt wreaking goddess only knows what havoc at home.

"Yes, unless that's an issue..."

My phone buzzes again, and I resist the urge to hurl it against the wall.

"Nope, not an issue. I can make that happen," I squeak, eyes darting back to my overflowing list. I'd planned to leave at five, grab cat food, then spend the evening alone with my thoughts, a cold gin and tonic, and one of the romcoms Netti sent me.

"Wonderful. I'll see you then," she says, and the line goes dead.

If I leave exactly on time, I'll have just enough time to swing by the grocer, feed Ginger, and make it to the lounge by seven.

I go to toss my phone in my purse, but the screen catches my eye—twenty-one missed text messages.

It *should* be easy to move on from Jett—he wasn't even that good a lover, for goddess' sake—if only he'd stop fucking texting me.

CHAPTER 3
ROSE

THREE WEEKS LATER

Throwing my purse onto the passenger seat, I sigh, close my eyes, and rest my head against the headrest as the roar of my magic settles into a low hum. My head feels foggy and my hands tremble as I pull the seatbelt across my chest, clicking it into place. After a night surrounded by so many people, I'm both drained and overstimulated.

Normally, I thrive on planning events and parties—being an emotional conduit witch—but the constant barrage of texts from my ex this past week has my adrenaline spiking, making it difficult to control my magic. I rub my temples and inhale deeply.

A month. That's how long it's been since I caught him backstage with another woman. At an event I planned. With one of his favorite bands. I never thought he'd cheat, but the image is burned into me: half-naked, tangled up behind instrument cases, her lipstick smeared down his neck like a brand—

No. I'm not going there. I won't let him ruin this gig. Ruin my career—the one I've bled, sweat, and clawed for. Years of school, building connections, grinding through every step. I won't let him ruin that too. On the night of our fucking one-year anniversary, no less.

Happy anniversary to me.

This is why I should've stuck to the plan: graduate, then make something of myself. Live my best life helping others. I wasn't supposed to meet him that last semester. Wasn't supposed to let anyone in. I was lonely, trying to fill the void in my chest I still can't explain. I thought Jett cared. Maybe even loved me, in his own way.

Now I know better. It was all a façade to worm his way into my connections. Maybe it was that way from the start. Maybe I was a fool, seeing something that wasn't there but that I wanted. Does it matter?

I pull out my phone, block his number, and delete the one-sided text chain.

My chest loosens, like I can finally breathe without that invisible weight pressing down. Even the knot between my brows eases. I should've listened to Netti—not just weeks ago, but months ago, when she flew in, took one look at him, and quietly warned me. She said something felt off, that I deserved better. That I should leave space for someone who could actually love me. I laughed her off, told myself she didn't understand him. Didn't get the moody, artistic energy I'd grown accustomed to.

But maybe... deep down, I knew she was right.

My lips tingle with a memory—not Jett's, but another man's. A kiss that stole my breath a year ago. A kiss I ran from out of fear. I was in my last year of college and wanted only freedom. So why does Carter Abernathy still haunt my every thought?

I have to get him out of my head.

The neon dash clock glares in the dark as I double check my seatbelt, shift into reverse, and pull out of the lot. Tonight is Wolflight's opening performance, and I've taken a side gig coordinating the event at Summerwind. It's a change of pace from the birthdays and banquets I've run at Greyhaven's event hall. The hall pays the bills, but it isn't my endgame. That's why I keep picking up side work.

Openings are my favorite—the magic of starting something new, of watching a dream come to life. And Angelique's lounge has been consuming every spare moment since her call weeks ago. I'm exhausted, but once the opening runs smoothly, it could open doors I've only dreamed of. Maybe then I'll finally put in my two weeks at the event hall and chase freelance work full-time. Travel the world, gig to gig.

That's been the dream since childhood. Nearly a year has passed since I graduated from Catoria University with my degree in Event Planning, and I've been working nonstop ever since—securing high-profile gigs at exclusive clubs nationwide. Jett hated that drive in me, said it didn't match his pace. At first, he seemed supportive, even when I was traveling for internships. I thought being an artist, he'd understand. That he'd want the same.

I sigh, pulling the tie from my hair and massaging my aching scalp before it spirals into a migraine.

His wandering eye—and other parts—should've been a warning. I'd caught him checking people out more than once. He always claimed it was artistic study for a new project. And I'd believed him.

Artistic study, my ass. More like practicing to be a cheating asshat.

Why didn't I use my magic? I could've read his emotions, uncovered the truth. But I have boundaries. Peering into someone's feelings without permission is a breach of trust. And magic isn't perfect—people can hide, lie, twist themselves into something they're not.

I trusted him.

And look where it got me.

I should've ended things before they became serious, but my career consumed me, and he was a comforting distraction from the emotional rollercoaster at the end of each day. I thought he knew me. I thought he understood my drive for freedom, creativity, and helping others. I never thought he'd do what he did.

Slamming on the brakes, my seatbelt locks painfully across my shoulder as a car blows through a red light. My heart pounds, skin damp with cold sweat as I struggle to steady my breath. A few seconds later and they'd have T-boned my brand-new-to-me sedan.

Maybe I am working too hard. But it isn't forever. Besides, I'm making people happy, using both my magic and the skills I've spent the last four years honing. I like my job, *and* I'm good at it. He certainly didn't complain when it got us into the hottest events in the country—or paid for our expensive trips.

Fuck that loser.

I jab the radio on, blasting my favorite pop-rock station, and continue down the lamplit road. I've lived in sprawling cities and tiny towns, but the suburbs suit me best. Big enough for my favorite shops, small enough that I can walk to work or downtown. On early evenings, I often do—though Summerwind sits across town, nearly a thirty-minute drive from home.

At least for the rest of the month, aside from food runs and picking up décor, I can my work my side gig from my favorite café downtown.

The drive feels like minutes, but the dashboard clock says otherwise. I pull into the driveway of the one-story house I'm renting. Small, one bedroom and bath, but a spacious living room and pre-furnished. Not knowing how long I'd stay in Greyhaven, I rented instead of buying. Still, I made it feel like home—Netti even flew in for a small party when I moved in to celebrate my new job. Almost a year ago now.

And here I am, stuck in the same routine. The very thing I swore I'd never settle for. I wanted adventure. I wanted to travel, to experience life. When did I trade that for a nine-to-five and side gigs just to keep the dream alive?

I put the car in park, grab my purse, and lock up. Solar lamps illuminate the small concrete walkway. On the other side of the door Ginger mewls, tiny paws thudding against the wood.

"I'm coming, Ginger." I dig through my purse until I find the key. But when I bend to unlock the door, I notice a folded square of paper shoved beneath it.

I scratch Ginger's head before picking it up. My vision swims, stomach knotting as I recognize Jett's chicken-scratch handwriting. Bracing against the doorframe, I read:

> *Baby girl, I know I messed up but don't ignore me.*
> *I miss you.*
> *Love, Jett*

Scowling, I crumple the paper, glance outside—nothing amiss—then slam the door and throw the deadbolt before tossing it into the cold fireplace.

Couldn't he take the hint? I'm done. And now he's resorting to shoving notes under my door?

I scoop Ginger into my arms, his soft fur warm against my cheek, his purr vibrating through me. All I want is to curl up and shut the world out, but his insistent nudging breaks me out of my spiral.

"I'm sure you're hungry," I murmur, setting him down on the tile. My own stomach growls as I open the fridge. The faint scent of this morning's coffee lingers in the air. "Looks like dinner for two. I worked through lunch."

Ginger meows, copper fur prickling with static as he weaves between my legs. I pull out what's left: sliced turkey, Colby Jack, avocado-oil mayo, a crusty loaf of bread, and a cold root beer—a sugary promise. From the cupboard, I grab Ginger's food. The metallic clang echoes softly, the hiss of the can opening sharp. I serve him first, then wash my hands. My root beer fizzes when I crack it open, the sweet carbonation a small reward.

"Ready for bed?" I ask as he licks his paws, tail swishing. He follows on my heels as I head to the bedroom.

Hand on the switch, I pause. Movement near the window.

"Who's there?" My voice cuts sharp as I flip the light on. But it's only the curtain, swaying in the breeze. A chill creeps down my spine as I snap the window shut, lock it, and tug the blackout curtain into place.

I must've left it open this morning.

With a steadying breath, I loosen the bun holding my dark auburn hair and let it fall down my back, the weight soothing as I massage my tired scalp. Maybe I'll take a vacation—somewhere sunny, a beach for a week or two—once this project is over.

CHAPTER 4
CARTER

The fender of my cruiser gleams a dark cerulean blue, like the sky at dusk, as I swipe the microfiber cloth over its polished surface. A year has passed since I stepped down as the pack's Alpha, and I've had more free time than I know what to do with.

You could find the witch. My wolf growls inside my head, magic stirring under my skin, begging to be let free.

"You'll have to be more specific." I straighten, stretching out my legs after crouching too long. "We know plenty of witches, and to my knowledge none are lost."

You know who I'm talking about.

"I'm not about to chase tail over a witch I met once, over a year ago, who hasn't spoken to me since." Who refuses to even acknowledge my existence. That hasn't stopped me from keeping tabs on her safety, though. From cheering her on from the sidelines. A deep longing tugs at my chest, but I ignore it, packing up the wax and tools and carrying them back into the garage.

She is ours.

"We don't own—" My phone buzzes in my pocket, and I sigh, grateful for the distraction. "Hello?"

"Carter? It's Josephine. Do you have a moment?"

The edge of anxiety in her tone sets off warning bells. Even my wolf goes quiet.

"Yeah, I'm just cleaning up. What's going on?" I wedge the phone between my ear and shoulder as I slot the detailing equipment into their containers. The garage door slides shut behind me with a soft thud, sealing out the sun's last rays and the crisp air.

"Well, I hate to bother you. I know so much has changed since you—"

"Josephine, it's fine. What's wrong?" I move into the kitchen, scrubbing my hands with Gojo, watching the grime swirl down the stainless-steel sink.

"It's Alexandria..." She sniffles, and my lips tug downward. "She's missing. But alive."

"Missing?" I grab a towel from the hook, drying my hands. "What do you mean missing *but alive*? How long has she been gone? Are you sure she's not just off with friends? She must be sixteen—seventeen now?"

"She's seventeen," Josephine confirms with a shaky breath. "But she hasn't gained full control of her wolf. You know how kids are at that age—hormones all over the place."

"Yes, I remember." I rub at my brow, memories of my brother and me brawling at that age surfacing. Our father always pushing us to dominate the wolf within.

I'll show you domin—

"Well, it's been a little over a week," Josephine continues.

"We thought she was staying with a friend. It's near the end of spring vacation and she's got a few more months of high school left. Normally she tells us, but she's been emotional, rebellious, pushing curfews. We were picking our battles. But no one has seen her in days. Then her friend Margaret told us Alexandria texted yesterday. Said she was safe, had found a part-time job... but wasn't coming home."

"Why didn't Margaret tell you sooner?" I pace, mind already racing through possibilities.

"I don't know. You know how teens are." Her voice cracks, sobs spilling through the line. "I just want my baby girl back, Carter. And I didn't know who else to ask. I thought... maybe now that you're not shouldering leadership of the pack, you could find her. Bring her home where she belongs."

My chest tightens as memories flash—my brother walking away from the pack, leaving me to follow in our father's footsteps. It had taken everything in me not to run too.

"I'll do what I can. Do you have any idea where she might have gone? Did she drive?" I rub at the back of my neck, dread whispering through every possibility. The worst—her losing control of her wolf, hurting innocents, and living scarred by it for forever. *If* she survived the shift back.

"All I have is the photo she sent Margaret. Not much else. We tried tracking her phone, but she turned the locator off. Her car's still in the driveway, so she can't have gone far... right?"

"Don't worry, Josephine. I'll find her. Text me the photo. In the meantime, see if Margaret can reach her again—any clue to where she is, or at least that she's okay. I'll find her."

"Okay. Thank you." She hangs up, and seconds later my phone pings with a photo notification.

I forward the image to my laptop. The screen flashes confirmation, but I linger, studying the picture. A seventeen-year-old with wavy brown hair and olive skin grins back at me, flashing a peace sign against a backdrop of some small-town street.

But in my mind, I don't see the teenager. I see the little girl she once was—three years old, swinging between her parents' arms as they walked her home.

With a sigh, I open the fridge, grab a chilled protein shake, crack the seal, and take a long swallow. The vanilla-sweet taste does nothing to chase off the weight pressing at the back of my mind. My feet carry me into the office, leather chair creaking as I sink down and roll forward until my knees bump the desk.

I should feel lighter. I'm not Alpha anymore, not the one shouldering every crisis. Connor carries that burden now—and he's damn good at it. Still... instinct doesn't fade so easily. Every face, every problem, every threat feels like it still ties back to me. Years of leading don't vanish just because you hand over the title.

Just because we're not Alpha in title doesn't make our role any less important. The pack still needs us.

The girl's image lingers, stirring an ache in my chest. Whatever she's gotten tangled up in, I can't ignore it. That's not who I am. Not who I'll ever be. My wolf paces beneath my skin, restless. Alpha or not, these people—this pack—will always be mine to protect.

"Where are you?" I pull the photo up full screen and zoom in. Blurry background. Damn teens and their fancy portrait modes. I toss it into a security imaging program, sharpening until the street signs and shops come into focus.

"Second Avenue and Lake Street. That really narrows it down," I mutter, rolling my eyes as the map loads hundreds of results. "Okay, let's try something else." Sliding along the photo, I trace the shop signs. "Café, Bakery, The Bookshop—"

They really know how to stand out, eh?

"Generic as hell," I say. "But—ah hah." Down the street, a woman carries a bag stamped with a cartoon pile of candy and Delilah's Divine Delights in looping script. I type it in.

A news article pops up: "Delilah's Divine Delights, Bringing Handmade Confections to Greyhaven for Twenty Years."

Greyhaven. Got you, little wolf pup. But why does that town sound so familiar?

I fire off a text to Josephine.

> I may know where she is. I'll check it out tomorrow and keep you updated.

Her reply comes quickly:

> Thank you, Carter. Just bring my baby girl home.

I pull up directions on my phone. Six hours. Greyhaven is six hours away. I groan and pinch the bridge of my nose. How did she get that far without her car in just a few days? Josephine wasn't clear on the timeline—maybe Alexandria left the first day, maybe she lingered before bolting. She could've run the whole way in wolf form. Or hitched a ride.

A teenage wolf with barely any control on the loose, or a teenage girl thumbing rides with strangers. I don't know which is worse.

Sighing, I lean back and drag my hands through my short black hair. A six-hour drive, if I'm lucky enough to find her right away. Greyhaven isn't huge, but it sits right outside of Clarksdale, and that city's population could swallow her whole. The photo is from today, but what if she's already moved on? No. Don't go there. Focus.

I finish the shake, rinse the bottle, and drop it in the recycling bin.

Moonlight ride?

The clock on my phone reads 6:30 p.m. If I leave now, I'll hit Greyhaven just after midnight—enough time to catch a few hours' sleep before starting the search.

I shrug into my leather jacket, throw toiletries and a few days' clothes into a duffle, and brew a quick cup of coffee. The rich aroma fills the kitchen as I down it in three gulps. In the garage, I hit the button for the door, reach for my helmet on the shelf—and pause.

The second helmet sits beside it, unused. I'd never let anyone else ride my bike, but when I bought it, something urged me to order a spare. My chest aches as I swipe both helmets, strapping one to the back of the seat.

Come on, Captain America.

I roll my eyes and swing onto the bike. The engine roars to life, humming steadily between my thighs.

"Let's go rescue a wolf pup."

CHAPTER 5
ROSE

I nibble on the back of my ballpoint pen as I sweep over the list of things I need to do today for the Wise Fox Lounge's grand opening. I know I should be working on this month's events for the city's event hall, but the lounge is constantly on my mind, and I still have an hour before I have to show up at work.

"Do you need another refill, miss?" I look up at the young barista, her golden curls pulled back in a bun, as she gestures to my empty cup.

"Oh, uh, yes please." My stomach growls audibly. "Another caramel macchiato and a BLT, lightly toasted, please."

"Would you like anything else?" She grabs my cup and smiles patiently.

"No, thank you."

A glance at my watch shows it's already half past ten. I've wasted nearly two hours this morning and haven't managed to do anything but scroll through social media, text Netti, and check in on my cat cam. Ginger had been sound asleep in the tree I ordered last week, his tail swishing as he dreamed.

The bell above the café door chimes. I shake my head and drag a finger down my to-do list. There's still time before the lounge's opening, but I like to be prepared with backup plans in case something goes wrong. Not that it will. The bakery I chose for the macarons is a family-owned business, always praised for its flavor and promptness. I've already explored catalog options, consulted a local florist, and just need to review the decoration details one last time with Angelique before finalizing the order. Fortunately, the lounge is fully furnished, eliminating the need to rent chairs and tables—one less thing to worry about.

My chest constricts, a chill running down my spine. I swivel in my seat, scanning the café. Only the barista and an elderly patron are here.

It's probably nothing. Just stress. And lack of decent sleep.

It couldn't be him.

My ex, stalking me.

I rub the back of my neck and stare out the window. Cars roll by; only a handful of pedestrians are out—two mothers pushing strollers, an elderly couple holding hands, a man turning the corner out of sight.

I push to my feet, chair scraping along the floor. My heart beats wildly as I stare at the narrow street between the bakery and the barbershop through the storefront window.

"Miss, are you alright?" the barista asks.

I turn. Both she and the elderly man are watching me.

"Yes, I'm fine. Sorry, I thought I saw something but it— never mind." I smile and sit back down, letting the warm sun streaming through the glass calm my nerves as I breathe deep.

It can't have been Jett. He has better things to do than stalk me. He has a job. Or at least, he did before we broke up. He never stayed anywhere long, always bailing when responsibility got too heavy.

My hand clenches, crumpling the paper to-do list. I smooth it flat again, eyes catching on the bakery line. I'll finish my coffee and brunch, then give them a call.

"Here you go, miss," the barista says, and I glance at her nametag. Alice. That's a nice name. She's been here since before I moved to town. If this is going to be my regular spot, it wouldn't hurt to be on a first-name basis.

"Thank you... Alice. My name is Rosemary, but you can call me Rose." I smile as I take the cup.

"Enjoy your food, Rose," she replies, turning away just as the bell above the café door chimes again.

This is the busiest I've ever seen it after the morning rush. Usually, I'm the only one here until—

"Rose?"

A deep, familiar voice rolls through me, and my magic sings in response, a euphoric rush lighting every nerve. I turn, brows furrowed.

"Carter? What are you doing here?"

"I could ask you the same thing. Boy, are you a sight for sore eyes." He beams, a dimple flashing in his cheek. "I hope I'm not interrupting."

His eyes stray to the list on the table, the sticky notes scattered around it, my neat row of pens and highlighters.

"No, not at all, please." I gesture to the chair across from me, my gaze locked on him. He slips off his leather biker jacket, folding it neatly over the back of the chair before sitting. Fitted jeans hug his thighs, and his dark grey shirt does little to hide the physique beneath.

"Hello." The barista is at our table again, batting her lashes at Carter. "Can I get you anything to drink?"

"Just a flat black," he says matter-of-factly.

My stomach twists in a jealous knot. I force myself to look back down at my list, but it only reminds me of the note I threw into the firepit last night. I have absolutely no reason to be jealous of Carter Abernathy. Sure, he's part of the Abernathy werewolf clan—brother to a billionaire CEO who just happens to be engaged to my best friend. And yes, we had a weekend fling over a year ago. But that was it. I had one more semester of college left, and neither of us wanted a long-distance relationship or to give up our lives, so we left it at that. No sad story. No messy breakup. Just a weekend of fun, a little steam blown off.

Or at least, that's what I told myself. Over and over until I believed it. Did I compare every man I met afterward to him? Possibly. Did I still wake up with vivid dreams of that weekend? Absolutely. But I never thought I'd see him again—except maybe at an event Netti invited me to, if I could get the time off.

"Rose?"

Carter places his hand over mine, and I jump, pulling back.

"I'm so sorry," I blurt, glancing up. Alice is already behind the counter, busy making coffee.

"You made a face and zoned out. Have you been sleeping?" His dark brows knit together over perfectly tan skin.

"Yes. Well, no. But that's beside the point." I grab my cup and take a long swig. The liquid scalds my tongue. He folds his arms across his chest, biceps bulging, a hint of ink peeking out from his sleeve.

"What's that?" I ask, gesturing toward his arm. I don't remember him having ink when we met.

"This?" He pushes the sleeve higher, revealing pine trees and a crescent moon. Heat pools low in my belly, memories flooding back—crisp air, a hotel in the woods, his mouth on mine.

"Just some art." Carter's nostrils flare, pupils dilating for half a second before he clears his throat, readjusts in his chair, and gestures to the table. "What's this?"

"This? Just work." I fiddle with my pens, lining them up.

"Is that why you're in town? Another gig?" He lifts a brow.

"Well, this particular job is, but I've also taken a year contract with the—actually, it doesn't matter. Why are *you* here? Don't you have 'fancy pack business'?" I make air quotes. I know his role is important, but I've never dug into the details. Anytime Netti brought him up, I skirted around the subject.

Alice reappears, lashes fluttering again as she hands Carter his drink.

"I'm here on pack business." He takes the steaming cup and pulls out a fifty. "I'll cover her tab. Keep the change."

I resist rolling my eyes at these stupidly rich werewolves and their antics.

"I have a big-girl job. I can pay for my own big-girl coffee," I protest.

"Why don't you calm down, kitten, and let someone take care of you for once."

"Why don't you tell me why you're in town." I bite my lip, grumbling. "And I'm not your kitten."

Why does his mere presence leave me hot, cold, and twisted up inside?

"Have it your way... kitten." Carter smirks, leaning forward, his knees brushing mine. "I'm here because I'm hunting down a wild wee beastie."

I release the breath I didn't know I was holding and roll my eyes.

"Carter, be serious." For once. His jovial, easygoing nature is impossible for me to read, and he's the only person I've ever met immune to my magic. Just being near him tangles me in feelings I don't have time for.

"I am serious. One of the pups—well, she's a teen, really— decided to run away earlier this week." His voice turns grave as he sips his coffee.

"What do you mean? Is she okay? Do you know why?" The hair on my arm rises.

"Something about chasing her dreams, getting out from under pack rules, living her own life. Typical teenager stuff. You'd know." He shrugs, but his eyes stay locked on me.

"Was that a jab at my age and life choices?" I bristle. "I'm serious, Carter. A missing teen isn't a joke."

"I never said it was." His tone is solemn. "If I didn't care, I wouldn't be here. But since you brought up age and life choices... well, you're what—" He smirks, that damned dimple flashing, ticking down fingers. "Thirty-two years younger than me?"

"Just because I'm younger doesn't mean I don't know what I'm doing. And didn't your brother say you wolf boys live longer but take longer to mature?"

"Touché, kitten."

"I told you to stop calling me that."

"Then look me in the eyes when you say it." His voice hardens with steel, and my face heats. I force myself to meet his gaze.

"How come you never returned my calls or texts that week?" he asks, his hand closing over mine.

"It was just one weekend. What does it matter?" I whisper,

staring at his large hand dwarfing my petite one. "That was a long time ago, and we've both moved on."

Liar. Liar. Liar. If I had truly moved on, why do I feel this way when he looks at me?

"I suppose we have." He drops my hand and leans back. The loss of his warmth is a cold bucket of water to my senses. "I'm here looking for the missing girl. Have you heard anything?"

"I have not." I run my finger around the rim of my cup before meeting his blue stare. "What makes you think she's here?"

"She texted one of her friends this picture yesterday." He pulls his phone from his pocket and angles the screen toward me. The girl has dark, wavy brown hair, an olive complexion, and wide brown eyes. Beyond her stretch nondescript shops and storefronts.

"How do you know that's here? That could be any small town."

"Except it's not." He zooms in and points to a woman carrying a bag. "See this? That shop's only location is here."

I try to focus on what Carter's pointing out, but all I can see is a figure in the background, leaning against a building. Jett.

Why would he be in this girl's selfie?

I drain the last of my coffee, staring at my now-cold sandwich. Appetite gone, I think of the teen—lost and alone.

"Aside from her being a runaway, what makes you so worried? You don't think there's foul play, do you?" I meet his cerulean-blue gaze, but he shakes his head.

"No, I don't suspect that. The problem is, teenage shifters often struggle with their emotions, and our magic is tied to them. So is our ability to shift. A rogue teen shifter without her pack can get into a lot of magical trouble."

The knot in my stomach eases, and I nod. Maybe it isn't Jett after all—maybe I'm just wound up and paranoid. The man's face is obscured, and anyone could be wearing jeans, a band shirt, and a baseball cap.

"Well, with your superior wolf-shifter senses, you'll find her in no time," I say, packing my things. Another hour gone, and if I'm going to get this opening done on time, I need a clear head.

"That's the problem." His eyes lock onto mine. "There are more than just shifters in this town. I've sensed witches, fae, even humans. Unless I'm practically breathing down her neck, I can't track her by scent alone."

"So... you need my help?" I arch a brow.

"I didn't ask for your help." His lips twitch into that almost-smile I've dreamed about too many nights.

"No, but you dropped this mission in my lap like a hot coal. You're in unfamiliar territory, chasing down a missing pack member. I've been here long enough to know the people and places. The question was implied." I cross my arms, ignoring the quickening of my pulse just from being this close.

"Netti always says you like making yourself indispensable." He leans back, smirk widening, the picture of infuriating confidence. "Go on. Admit it. You like helping people."

"We barely know each other. What could you possibly know about what I like and don't?" I roll my eyes, though heat curls low in my belly at the challenge in his voice.

"I know enough." His grin softens slightly, making my heart ache. He spreads his arms wide. "I know you're a fighter, that you don't give up easily, and you like a challenge."

"I don't see how I can help. I don't know the first thing about shifter pups." I stand, slinging my purse and laptop bag over my shoulder. His words hit me harder than I expected.

Was I that easy to read? What had Netti told him? "Thank you for covering my brunch. You really didn't have to."

I turn to go, but his hand wraps gently around my wrist. I crane my neck up to meet his gaze. Heat radiates off him, cedarwood, vanilla, and bourbon wrapping around me.

"Rose." His voice is low, almost a whisper. His eyes drop to my lips before returning to mine. Then he lets go, stepping back, shaking his head. "I'm sorry. I just... could really use your help."

It takes every ounce of self-control not to close the space between us. Even with Jett gone, I'm not ready to throw myself back into dating. Especially not with Carter Abernathy—the man who stirs a storm in me I can't name.

"I'll help you." Goddess help me, I hope I don't regret this. I swore I'd start saying no more often, but some reckless part of me wants more time with him—even if it means chasing down a lost pup.

"You will?" His eyes light up like a puppy being offered a bone. I suppress a laugh and hold up a hand.

"I'll keep an eye out, ask my contacts at the clubs and para-normal hangouts if they've seen her. It's the least I can do. But I have work too."

"Thank you." He pulls me into a brief hug before stepping back. "Text me if you hear anything. My number hasn't changed. I'm staying at Lana Hotel."

He grabs his jacket and strides out the door to a sleek blue motorcycle parked at the curb. I watch as he dons his helmet, swings onto the saddle, revs the engine, and disappears down the street.

CHAPTER 6
CARTER

*W*hy *did you leave when you could clearly smell she wanted us?*

"She doesn't want us—or a long-distance relationship. How many times do we have to go over this?" My blood heats at the thought of her. Not a day has gone by without something reminding me of Rose.

I pull the bike to a stop outside Delilah's Divine Delights. The sweet scent of chocolate and sugar wafts into the street. Even a human without supernatural senses would catch it.

But we aren't long-distance right now.

"I don't want just another weekend fling." I strap my helmet to the seat, my finger tracing the curve of its feminine twin before pulling away. "Besides, we're here to find the girl, not get in bed with the witch."

Who says it has to be a fling?

I shade my eyes, scanning up and down the street. Reaching for my magic, I draw in the air, but just like before, the jumble of scents makes it impossible to pick the shifter pup out.

You'd find Rose in a crowd. She's ours, Carter. Don't let her slip away again.

A phantom trace of blueberries and cream still clings to my skin from that brief touch earlier, fueling every instinct in me to claim her.

I'd sensed it a year ago, the moment she and her friend Netti walked into that conference center. My wolf went feral, and if it hadn't been for my brother's scarf around her neck, I would've lost control. I hadn't felt that wild since I was a teenager.

"Fate may have marked her as ours, but I won't force her into anything. We don't even know if she feels the tug of the bond the way we do."

She wants us.

I ignore him, grasp the cool knob, and step inside. The street smelled like sugar; the shop is a diabetic coma waiting to happen.

It's a child's dream brought to life: rainbow candy stripes glitter across the walls, glass jars overflow with bright sweets, polished shelves gleam under too-bright lights. The air hums with a giddy, cloying euphoria. Behind the counter, a plump, middle-aged woman beams, demi-pointed ears barely peeking through curly grey hair. Her ruffled pink A-line suit makes her look as if she belongs to this candy-coated wonderland.

"Well, hello there, dearie." She wipes down a gleaming bronze register—the only thing in the room not dripping with sugar. "How can I help you?"

"I'm looking for a girl—"

Her brows shoot up, lips pressing thin.

"We aren't that kind of establishment, shifter. I don't know where you're from but—" Her ears flush bright pink as she glances around the empty shop.

"I'm *not* here for that. I have reason to believe a young member of my pack, the daughter of a friend, was recently in or near your shop."

"I get plenty of young folk coming through for candy. My treats are famous for their... positive side effects." She plants her hands on her hips.

I bite back my impatience, gesturing to the rows of jars. "I'm well aware of your candy and its magical properties. You've got an impressive following from both supernaturals and humans."

She preens under the compliment. In my experience, most fae—especially halflings, as I suspected she was—are vain about their reputations.

"And why do you think she came here?"

"She sent a photo yesterday from a street nearby. One of the people in the background was carrying a bag with your shop's logo." I pull out my phone, zooming in on the image. "I can't say for certain she came in, but kids and candy—it's a magnet."

The woman studies the photo, lips pressed tight. Finally, she nods. "Yes, I do believe I saw her just the other day. A beautiful creature, polite too. She bought a small bag of hard candies and went on her way."

"Do you know where?" I step closer, eager.

"Sir, I rarely leave my shop. I only saw her turn left when she left. That's all. You might try the paranormal hangouts. I hear the new club sometimes lets the younger ones in until nine."

"Thank you. I haven't tried there yet." I turn toward the

door, then pause. "Do you happen to have anything blueberry flavored?

"Blueberry? Of course. I've got lollies, saltwater taffy, licorice ropes—"

"I'll take some of each, please." I lay a bill on the counter.

Her eyes light up as she bustles around, filling a clear bag with sweets in every shade of blue and purple.

I can still see Rose's eyes the moment she spotted the blueberry donuts in that little coffee shop the weekend we met—bright, unguarded, sparking with joy. Her laugh, the sugar dust clinging to her lips. She'd leaned close and whispered, conspiratorial, that blueberry was her greatest weakness, and I'd quietly decided to remember it forever.

A year later, I can only hope her tastes haven't changed. Because mine sure as hell haven't.

CHAPTER 7
ROSE

I pull up to the nearly completed Wise Fox Lounge and kill the engine, the hum of the car fading into the quiet afternoon street. My heart thuds against my ribs like it's trying to make a break for it. Leaning toward the rearview mirror, I touch up the sharp line of my winged eyeliner and smooth a hand over the loose waves of my dark auburn hair. No smudges. No stray strands. I have to look composed, even if inside I'm anything but.

This is it. The biggest gig of my career since graduation. For Angelique DeThistle herself—*the* Angelique DeThistle— renowned owner of not just this lounge but half a dozen other hot spots in the supernatural world. The call she'd made weeks ago still replays in my mind like a dream. Me. Of all the event managers she could've chosen, she'd asked for me. I should've said no, considering the mountain of work at the event hall and the tail end of another project already eating my nights alive. But how could I? This wasn't just a job. This was *the* opportunity—the kind that cracks open doors to national gigs, maybe even international ones, if I play my cards right.

And so I've lived and breathed this project for weeks: sketches, proposals, sleepless nights perfecting details. We'd met briefly twice for lunch to go over ideas. Otherwise, every free moment not taken up by the city's event hall has gone into making the Wise Fox's grand opening flawless.

With a deep breath, I slide out of the car, tugging my pencil skirt straight before reaching for my purse. Tilting my chin, I glance at the club's sign catching the sunlight, its looping script promising decadence even before it's lit. In two weeks, that sign will glow neon violet and indigo, summoning guests like moths to a flame. For now, it draws curious stares, as though the building itself whispers of secrets waiting inside.

The lounge is meant to be a haven for the supernatural— and for the humans privy to our world. I'd have to ask Angelique what the plan was for those humans who might be drawn to it. Would there be spells to deter them? Or would they be allowed inside, glamoured to see other patrons in humanoid form? I've heard of clubs across the country taking different stances, since not everyone knows magic exists.

The heavy double doors are propped open, faint music spilling out. I inhale, steady the flutter in my stomach, and step inside, heels clicking against the polished floor.

"Hello?" My eyes adjust as I walk further into the dim space. Low tables with plush blue velvet benches line the edges of the room. A stage anchors the back, ringed by a wooden dance floor. To the left, a bar stretches wall to wall, polished wood gleaming, shelves already half stocked with bottles and crystal. Behind it, a portly man with ruddy cheeks and peppered grey hair waves as he unpacks tumblers.

"Hello there. I'm looking for Angelique," I say, returning his wave. "I'm Rose. She asked me to meet here—"

"Yes, you must be the event coordinator. My name's Charlee." He gestures to the room. "She should be back any minute to show you the changes. I'm sure it looks a lot different from the last time you were here."

I set my purse on a nearby table and look up at the painted ceiling, dotted with thousands of glittering stars. Constellations sweep overhead, dancing across the roof. More than I imagined walking in.

"Yes, quite a bit different. Last time it was little more than bare walls and a dream. I'm surprised it looks so... finished." Relief loosens the knot in my chest. A part of me had feared we'd still need to rent furniture, but now it's clear the grand opening will run far more smoothly than I'd expected.

"Angelique leaves no room for error." Charlee shrugs, still unpacking. "She wanted the remodel done early so you'd have time to work your magic."

"No kidding. I thought I'd be scrambling to make this place presentable, but it almost looks like we could open tonight without half the plans I've made." I tug my notepad from my purse, already jotting ideas.

"Now, where would be the fun in that?"

I nearly jump out of my skin at the sound of her voice.

"Angelique!" I whirl around, smiling despite myself at the beautiful woman framed in sunlight, her aura as golden as the light behind her.

"Hello, Rosemary. I'm so glad you could make it. Quite different from the last time you were here, isn't it?"

"It looks better than I could've imagined. It's a pleasure to see you again." I incline my head.

"The pleasure is all mine, my dear." She steps forward. I

extend a hand, but she bats it away, pulling me into a deep hug. My magic hums at the contact, a rush of her emotions sweeping through me before she pulls back and gestures for me to follow. Some people project so strongly it only takes a brush of contact to feel them.

"This is only a taste of the magic that's changed since your last visit, my little witch." Angelique's heels click like a metronome as she sweeps ahead, her voice lilting with excitement. "You gave me so many ideas at our last luncheon!"

"Yes, about those..." I snatch up my purse and hurry after her, trying not to trip over her breakneck pace. She waves to Charlee as we breeze through a wide archway that, last I remember, led into one of the smaller ballrooms.

Only—it wasn't a ballroom anymore.

The music from the lounge fades as we step into a hallway lined with tall arches. Beyond each opening stretches a room, every one of them dressed in a different theme. I pause at each doorway, admiring the setting and decorations. How had she managed to pull all this together so fast?

I slow, blinking. "Wait. You took my suggestion and turned the ballroom into smaller rooms?" When we'd gone to lunch, I'd mentioned using blue as a theme for the grand opening because of its emotional impact. I'd also suggested having separate spaces for people who wanted the lounge atmosphere without being swallowed by the throbbing main room. I never expected her to implement all of it.

"Exactly!" Angelique beams, sweeping an elegant hand down the corridor. "Intimate conference spaces—perfect for small parties, private gatherings, or patrons who want the energy without the chaos. I even had speakers installed so they can hear the live music."

I shake my head, still absorbing it all. "I... should remind you, I'm not really an interior designer. I just plan events. Those ideas we discussed at lunch were just that—ideas. I'm only here as the grand opening coordinator."

"Oh, please." She scoffs lightly, glancing over her shoulder. "I've never seen someone with such a sharp eye for color. Your skills are being wasted if you don't use them."

Heat creeps into my cheeks. My fingers twitch toward the hem of my blouse, but I curl them into a loose fist. "I only expanded on what you'd already started. You're the one with the vision."

"Nevertheless," Angelique says with finality, striding ahead, "it was your suggestions that pushed me to do it."

Before I can protest further, she pushes open a door, and we step into a gleaming kitchen. Stainless steel counters line the walls, packed with ovens, stovetops, and a massive sink. A walk-in freezer gleams at the far end like a vault.

Angelique claps her hands together. "Of course, it won't be fully operational for the grand opening, but eventually I want full service here—light food, appetizers, something to keep guests lingering. Remind me, darling, what were our catering options again?"

I flip to the next page in my notebook. "Padre Campos is providing sandwiches and charcuterie boards, and we managed to score macarons from Maisel's."

Her mouth ticks up, head tilting in approval. "Yes, good. We'll handle drinks here. Charlee assures me the first shipment of alcohol has arrived, along with most of the glassware. What do you think of the cerulean blue?

Cerulean. The same shade as Carter's bike. The same shade as his eyes.

My stomach flips. I plaster on a smile and try to think of anything but the wolf. "It's as cozy as a fox's den," I say, clearing my throat. "A color known both for its calming ability and for sparking creativity. Exactly the mood the lounge sets, as we envisioned. It's fresh but familiar, especially compared to the trend of burgundy and gold. I think it'll get people talking."

"Indeed. You have a sharp eye for color theory, Rose. Keep it up and you'll never find yourself without work again." She straightens a pot on a shelf, then glances back. "And the decorations?"

"I've spoken to two local florists about bouquets. I still need to pick up the ordered décor from the supply store, but everything will be ready well in advance. Flowers and food will be delivered that morning."

"And the music?" She crosses her arms, acrylic nails tapping her sleeves.

"The band confirmed for opening night. They'll rehearsal the night before for sound check. I've already let Charlee know where to set up if I'm not here when they arrive."

"Fantastic. I knew you wouldn't disappoint me. I have very important guests flying in for the grand opening." We exit another door on the far side of the kitchen, coming out behind the bar. "As much as I'd love to stay and chat, I have a client dinner. Please do another walk-through, take notes as needed, and inform Charlee if you require anything. Otherwise, I'll see you the evening before the grand opening.

She turns on her heel with a wave. I sigh, shoulders sagging.

"You must've done something to really impress her," Charlee remarks. "She doesn't usually hand over the reins. I've been with her nearly fifteen years, and she's always the one calling the shots."

"I just hope this event is everything she's dreamed of and more." Pride swells in my chest, my lips curling into a smile. I glance at my watch and blink—it's already half past three. "I'm going to do another walk-around before heading out. Are you locking up soon?"

"I'll be here a few more hours. Shipment came this morning, and I need to finishing setting up the bar so I can get to other things this week. Holler if you need anything." Charlee hefts a crate of wine bottles and disappears down a stairwell leading to the basement.

"Thank you," I murmur to his retreating steps, though my voice falters as a sudden chill slides down my spine. My steps stall. The room looks perfectly ordinary, but the prickling at the back of my neck says otherwise. I swear it feels as though someone—or something—is watching me.

Forcing a breath, I shake my head and press on. The newly renovated back hall stretches ahead, each alcove dressed in careful detail. I slow my pace, jotting notes as I go, but my pen feels heavy in my hand, my focus tugged by that lingering unease.

Get a hold of yourself, Rose. There's no one here. You just need more sleep.

I walk the length of the hallway, peering into each doorway until I reach the last room, where enchanted sconces flicker against carved wood and velvet lounges. Mauve and bronze hues wrap the space in a muted glow, the low table arranged as though expecting company. My gaze drifts to the far wall. Heavy drapes conceal what looks like a window, though even from here I can feel it—an odd magical pull, beckoning me closer.

Crossing the room, my fingers caress the velvet before tugging it aside. Sunbeams spill in, motes of dust suspended mid-breath. But it isn't the outside world I see. The glass hums faintly with magic, showing a forest of towering oaks, their leaves aflame in oranges and reds. The air itself seems to shift, crisp autumn coolness brushing my skin despite the lounge's warmth. An enchanted window. Angelique has really outdone herself.

Despite the wonder, unease clings sharp and insistent. I let go, and the curtain falls shut with a heavy whoosh. Darkness rushes back in, and it takes several long heartbeats for my eyes to adjust.

"You definitely need sleep, Rose." I turn toward the kitchen, jotting a note to ask Angelique which coven handled the spell-work on the windows—and what wards were in place.

"I'm all done here," I call to Charlee, who's perched precariously on a tall ladder, stocking bottles in a dozen shades of blue behind the bar.

"Oh, good. I was about to send a search party for you. Thought maybe you'd fallen prey to one of the rooms. She's going to put half the patrons to sleep with how comfortable some of that Italian furniture is." He chuckles, climbing down and dusting off his hands.

"It's going to be such a unique experience." I slip my notepad into my purse and hitch the strap higher on my shoulder, my gaze sweeping the details once more. A smile tugs at my lips. "I know I'm just here to help with the opening, but honestly? I'm in awe of what she's pulled together."

He gives a quiet laugh, leaning against the doorway. "From what she told me, half these ideas started with that luncheon you two had. I can see why she said you've got a gift—for people, for creating an atmosphere. It shows."

Heat creeps into my cheeks at the compliment. I look away, tucking a strand of hair behind my ear. "That's very kind of you to say." Adjusting my purse strap, I force a lightness into my tone even though my heart thuds harder than it should.

"Thanks for letting me get the last details down. This won't be the last time you're stuck seeing me."

"You're welcome anytime. I'll be here pretty much every day, and the door's always open. Oh, before I forget—" He ducks behind the bar and pulls out a folded piece of paper. "Some young man stopped by while you were in the back and dropped this off for you."

Excitement bubbles in my chest. Had Carter stopped by with more information? But why wouldn't he just text me—and how would he even know where I'd be? Still, I'd be lying if I said he hadn't lingered at the edge of my thoughts all day: the warmth of his hand on mine, the wondering if I'd been too rash walking away from a long-distance chance with him.

I take the note from Charlee and unfold it eagerly—only to feel my elation burst like a bubble. Not Carter's neat script, but Jett's hurried scrawl. My stomach knots. I crumple the paper and shove it into my purse, heat burning down my neck as my magic flares with anger.

Who does he think he is? It was bad enough he left notes at my house, but showing up at my new job? That's a step too far.

"Everything alright?" Charlee asks, eyebrows furrowed, his voice edged with fatherly concern from the top of the ladder.

"I'm fine. Just... not who I was expecting." I inhale through my nose, exhale through my mouth.

"I remember faces. If you don't want him coming around, he won't get access." The look he sends me is reassuring. Calming. I don't think Jett would hurt me—he just wants the connections I have. But he should've thought of that before getting into a lip-locking match with—

"You know what, Charlee? That would really help."

"Do you want me to walk you out?" He climbs down again, steady and solid.

My first instinct is to refuse. But then I remember the note under my door, the cracked window, and that feeling of being watched.

I'm exhausted. My nerves are fried. And I still have a dozen things to do today. The last thing I want is a confrontation with Jett.

"If it's not too much trouble, I'd appreciate that."

CHAPTER 8
CARTER

Carter, what if the girl has moved on? You of all people should know a lone wolf without their pack can lose their humanity. Remember when we had to deal with Alistair—

"Quiet," I growl. Of course I remember. Alastair had lost his wife in childbirth and left the pack to find himself. Instead, he let grief consume him and became more beast than man. It took six of my best warriors to hunt him down.

With a sigh, I lean over the hotel desk, crossing off another shop on the map I printed in the lobby last night. Since the candy store, the pup's trail has gone cold. No word to her family. No word to her friends.

My gaze flicks to the cellophane-wrapped bag of candies beside my silent phone. Still no contact from Rose.

I won't give up.

Perhaps you should text her.

"Why don't you focus on finding our missing pack member

instead of worrying about my love life." Closing my eyes, I pinch the bridge of my nose.

This was supposed to be simple. Get to town. Find the kid. Bring her home. I wasn't expecting the trail to vanish. I wasn't expecting to run into *her*—the woman who hasn't left my thoughts or dreams since that one weekend over a year ago.

Maybe she's thinking about us?

"She's moved on. We're no good for her anyway. She's got a budding career ahead of her, and what do we have?"

A sweet bike, sharp jawline, and washboard abs.

"Really? Washboard abs? That's your best?" I roll my eyes.

Your best.

"Need I remind you my attributes are yours? We've got work to do." Tapping the pen against my temple, I scan the map again.

Where would the pup have gone?

The candy store owner had mentioned some clubs in town. Maybe Rose would know which ones.

Before I can second-guess myself, I snatch up my phone. The screen lights, unlocking with a quick face scan. Rose's name glows at the top of my contacts, and my thumb hovers there, useless, for a long moment.

What the hell are you waiting for?

I could type out the words, make it about the missing girl. Pretend I just need her help. But we both know I don't. I've tracked harder trails with less.

So why does my chest tighten at the thought of her voice? Why does every excuse sound hollow when the truth is simpler, rawer, and far more dangerous?

I don't want just her help. I want her. Another hour. Another night. Another damn chance.

But how do I ask without sounding desperate? Without admitting it's not the mission that keeps me circling back—it's her.

"I think I need some coffee." I grab my leather jacket from the back of the chair.

We brewed coffee this morning. It's sitting cold on the nightstand.

"Exactly. Nothing like a hot cappuccino. Besides, we're not making much progress here." I fold the map, slip it into my pocket, and grab my keys.

You're just avoiding the real problem.

"The real problem is that we're no closer to finding the girl."

***

The scent of freshly ground coffee hits me as soon as I step into the café, but my attention is immediately drawn to the brunette waiting in line at the register.

Rose.

I walk toward her, watching her every move, every breath. Her dark brown hair is pulled back into a ponytail, and she's dressed in a cream blouse and dark blue slacks. She glances over her shoulder through the front window, shifting her weight between her feet. Her usual berry-and-creme scent is laced with sour anxiety.

"Hey, Rose," I say, reaching out to touch her shoulder.

She jumps nearly out of her skin, whirling around with a clenched fist poised to strike.

"Holy Saint Magnolia," she swears, her face softening as her cheeks flush pink. "Carter."

"The one and only. Though I've been told I bear an uncanny resemblance to my twin, Connor." I raise a brow, nodding at her still-clenched fist. "You okay, kitten?"

"I thought I told you to stop calling me that." She turns away and steps forward in line.

I lean down, my voice brushing her ear. "Why would I stop when it gets such a reaction from you?"

Her breath hitches, and it takes everything in me not to press my lips to the column of her neck.

"Actually, I came down for a proper cup of coffee. The hotel brew leaves much to be desired," I explain.

So does sleeping in a king-size bed by ourselves.

"It had nothing to do with trying to run into me again?" She lifts her eyes to mine, and the tug in my chest is sharp, familiar—the same pull I'd felt the first time we met. What I wouldn't give to know what she's thinking right now.

"Darling, I'd never object to running into you, planned or otherwise, but no. You're a grown woman with a career and schedule of your own. I'm here on a mission." I nod toward the register as she turns.

"I'd like a caramel cappuccino to go, please," she says to the barista.

"Make that two," I add, handing over a twenty. "Keep the change."

"Carter." She presses her lips together as we find a seat to wait.

"To make up for startling you. Next time you can pay." Smirking, I wink at her.

She glances out the window again, then traces absent-minded patterns through a ring of condensation left on the table.

"Rose, what's going on?"

"Nothing."

"Rose." I cover her hand with mine. "You don't have to talk

about it if you don't want to. But I'm here if you need an ear. Or claws and fangs."

Her lips twitch into the faintest smile. "It's just an ex. Nothing I can't handle."

"You can do all things," I say softly, "but you don't have to do everything alone. Netti would kill me if I let anything happen to her best friend."

"He just—" Her voice cuts off, thick with emotion. Tears shimmer at her lashes.

Red-hot anger burns in my chest. A million scenarios run wild in my head, each worse than the last. She deserves the world. Whatever some lowlife did to hurt her—

"Be careful—they're hot!" The barista sets two steaming paper cups on the table. Rose pulls her hands into her lap.

"Rose, I swear if he—" I growl, my wolf prowling beneath my skin.

"He's not dangerous. Just dumb. I don't know what I ever saw in him." She props her elbows on the table, fingers threading through the hair escaping her ponytail. "We broke up over a month ago, after I caught him with some blonde bimbo on our anni—actually, it doesn't matter."

"Do you…" I clear my throat, ignoring the bitter sting of jealousy. "Do you still have feelings for him?"

"No!" The word cracks like a whip, magic sparking in the air. Her hair tie snaps, hair spilling loose, and both lids pop off our coffees. Her eyes go wide, transfixed on the upturned lids. "I'm sorry—I haven't lost control of my magic like that in a long time. Strong emotions sometimes…"

"I'm sorry for bringing it up."

She shakes her head, blowing steam from her coffee. Hair frames her heart-shaped face. "It's not your fault. And to answer your question, no. I don't have feelings for him. Not anymore. I want nothing to do with him, but he can't seem to see that."

If he doesn't take the hint, we'll give him one he won't forget.

"Well, I'm here if you need me." I take a sip, savoring the caramel espresso. "Looks like I'll be in town longer than expected."

"No luck with the girl?"

"None. I checked a few shops near her last known whereabouts, but the trail went cold. With all the scents and wards in town, I can't even track her in wolven form."

"Well, I took the afternoon off from the event center, and I could really use some company. I met most of the shop owners when I first moved here. We could ask around." She gives me a shy smile, shoulders lifting in a shrug.

"I'd really appreciate that."

***

The sun is nearly setting when we exit the twelfth shop in this part of town. Two owners said they'd seen a girl matching her description running with a group of teens—but that was three days ago.

Rose stifles a yawn and stretches. She looks tired, but some of her usual glow has returned.

"I'm sorry I've kept you all day on this fruitless mission."

"It hasn't been a complete waste. I've got that couple who wants to rent the hall for their vow renewal ceremony and a potential clue that your missing girl is still in town." She smiles, gesturing to the bags in my arms loaded with cold-cut sandwiches and little bags of chips. "Plus, free dinner."

"You rescued their puppy two weeks ago. They were dying to pay you back. That doesn't count."

"What good is magic if I can't use it to help someone every

once in a while?" She looks at me, chin tilted in that way that makes her eyes shine.

"Magic or not, you'd go out of your way to help anyone. That's just who you are." I lift a hand, tempted to tuck a stray strand of hair behind her ear—but let it fall.

Her cheeks flush a beautiful pink as she drops her gaze. "I just like helping people."

"Well, I appreciate you. Do you want to find somewhere to sit and eat?"

"I'm sure you're exhausted and have other obligations. I can just eat when I get home." Her eyes flick to my pocket as it buzzes again. My phone's been vibrating with calls and texts for the last two hours. I'd checked briefly to make sure it wasn't urgent, but nothing was about the girl. I need to respond, but right now, Rose takes priority.

"They can wait a little longer. At least let me walk you to your car."

"Oh, no need. I walked to the café this morning. The house I'm renting is just a few blocks away."

"You want to walk home, by yourself, in the dark?" I stop and stare at her.

"This is the suburbs. And a small one at that. Netti's computer-freak brother already scoped the crime rates before she gave me her official blessing to move here." She crosses her arms, one eyebrow arched in the glow of the streetlamp.

"With a crazy ex who may or may not be stalking you?"

She sighs and throws her hands up. "Fine, wolf boy, you win. Walk me home." She lifts a finger. "But that's it. No funny business. No Captain America swooping in to save the day."

Wolf boy? Who is she calling wolf boy?

"Roger that. No funny business." I smirk, keeping pace as

she heads down the sidewalk. "And Captain America doesn't swoop—he walks with swagger and class."

We turn, walking side by side beneath the streetlamps. Soon we've left the commercial strip behind for a row of Cape Cod-style houses painted in shades of tan, beige, and blue. I glance at the woman beside me, and despite spending the entire afternoon together, I can't shake the sense something heavier lingers with her. There are faint blue shadows under her eyes, and her glow has dimmed—it's more than just working too hard.

The sun is nearly gone when Rose stops and gestures toward a cheery house, her car parked in the driveway, warm light glowing from the windows.

"Do you always leave the lights on?" I hold out an arm and stop her from moving closer. What if her ex tried to break in? I'd ring his neck.

She pats my forearm reassuringly before stepping around me. "It's fine, Carter. I leave it on for Ginger. When I first moved here, I adopted him. Well, he kind of adopted me. Sometimes I stay out late working, and I don't want him to get lonely, so I leave the kitchen light on." She hands me one of the two bags of food. "Are you gonna be alright getting back to the café for your bike?"

I survey her house one last time, reluctant to shake the feeling that something isn't right, then force a smile. "I'm a wolf shifter, remember? The night is my territory, basking in the moonlight—"

"You mean howling at the moon? When you turn all hairy with sharp teeth?" She gestures at me head to toe.

"No, darling." I inch closer until her warmth brushes against mine, pressing a chaste kiss to her temple and whisper, "I have control over myself and my wolf—even in the dark."

She inhales sharply, perfume wrapping around me, tongue darting out to wet her lower lip. It's all I can do not to crush her against me the way I've imagined nearly every night since that first weekend. Instead, I step back. "Good night, Rose."

Her fingers fumble with the hem of her shirt, and her scent shifts, desire sparking through the air. My restraint frays. I know it's time to leave. Being near her clouds my mind, drags me back to that first night.

I wave, turning down the sidewalk, but pause in the shadow of the neighbor's tree until she's safely inside. Her scent—berries and cream—still clings to me, each step back toward the café prickling my instincts.

We should go back to her.

"We already spent the entire afternoon together."

Something isn't right, Carter.

"I know. Leaving our mate by herself is never right." I glance back at her house. "She wants space. She's been on her own this long. She'll be fine." The words taste false.

A whine echoes in my head.

"Fine. We'll scope out the perimeter."

I wolf down my food, toss the wrappers in a bin, and let my magic stretch. Dropping to all fours, I pad into my wolven form. The world sharpens: scents crisper, colors brighter under the moonlight. I swing my head left and right as I lope back toward her house.

Her scent clings to everything—from her car handle to the walkway, lingering sweet on the air. Her magic hums, its signature wrapping the house in faint protection.

"See? Everything's fine," I whisper. But then, rounding the north side where the shutters are drawn, another scent cuts through: magic, sharp and acidic, laced with cheap men's cologne and stale alcohol.

My hackles rise. I sniff along the ground until I find it—a half-buried bundle of twigs and feathers bound by twine. Whatever it is, I don't want it anywhere near my witch. I clamp it in my jaw and carry it far, dumping it unceremoniously in an alley.

Then I return, circling once before curling beneath her window. I rest my head on my paws, ears pricked.

Just for tonight, I remind myself. Just to make sure that bastard doesn't come back.

CHAPTER 9
ROSE

With the sun's rays streaming through the window, my sleep is interrupted by Ginger, who has planted himself on my chest and started kneading with his tiny paws. I sit up, yawning wide, and scratch his soft little head.

"Alright, I'm up. I'm up. I know you want breakfast."

He pads after me on silent feet as I open a can of his favorite food and dump it into his tray before switching on the coffee machine. For the first time in weeks, I wake without that tightness in my chest—or the sense that someone is watching me.

Magic at my fingertips, I levitate my favorite mug, catching the glint of sunlight on the rim. The rich scent of brewing coffee fills the air as I pop in a pod. Back in my bedroom, I slip into casual business clothes and catch my reflection in the mirror.

I'm thinner than the last time I really looked, but there's color in my cheeks again.

Maybe being around the wolf is bringing you back.

"No. I don't need anyone but myself." I pinch my cheeks, brush my hair back into a ponytail, and walk back to the kitchen. I need to make a few arrangements for the upcoming opening before heading into the office. A glance at my watch shows I'm an hour ahead of schedule—enough time to confirm orders before diving into the bustle of town.

The machine beeps, and I pull the mug free, setting it gently on the counter. I reach for the cream, twist the cap, and nearly gag as the acrid stench of rotten milk hits me.

"Of course." I glare at the label. Two weeks expired. *Has it really been that long since I went grocery shopping?*

I shove the fridge closed and lean against it, irritation twisting in my stomach. Busy, distracted—sure. But letting something this simple slip? It feels like a reflection of everything else I've been letting slide. Maybe taking on the lounge's opening was more than I could chew.

I yank open the pantry and dig, finally finding the creamer tucked behind the oatmeal. A quick shake, a twist of the lid—and only a sad dusting of powder clings to the bottom.

"Perfect." I toss it into the trash with more force than necessary.

The memory blindsides me. Jett, smirking as he dumped the last spoonful into his mug and shoved the container back, practically empty. My jaw tightens. He must've left this here, and I hadn't even noticed until now—too busy boxing up his crap, too busy trying not to break.

Netti had come the next day after I called her, calm and steady as we folded, taped, and labeled every box. I'd wanted to hex him into oblivion. Instead, I returned it all, neat and intact. And now, here I am, craving coffee with nothing but the stale taste of regret—and missing my best friend.

Netti's with her boyfriend's wolf shifter pack now, working as a healer. Perhaps when the club opening is over, I'll take a week off to visit her.

Sighing, I glance down at Ginger. "Well, change of plans. Looks like I'm going to the store. Phone calls will have to wait."

He looks up, lets out a disgruntled meow, then dives back into his food as if annoyed that my spoiled milk dilemma interrupted his breakfast.

So much for being ahead of schedule.

Five minutes later, I pull into the grocery lot and cut the engine. Out of the corner of my eye, a small wolf darts around the side of the building.

That's strange. I don't usually see wolves in town—and hardly any stray dogs since I've moved here.

Could it be the girl Carter's looking for?

I shake my head and step inside. I should probably grab some other staples while I'm here, but I don't have time to linger—not after spending yesterday afternoon with Carter. My schedule at the hall isn't fixed, but I still need to email clients and arrange a pickup for the lounge decorations. My stomach growls.

That settles it. Nothing was going to get done without caffeine and carbs. I make quick work of filling my cart with snacks, creamer, a few freezer meals, and a gallon of double chocolate fudge ice cream before heading to the register.

"Did you find everything you were looking for?" the teen at the counter drones, her dark hair and kohl-lined eyes reminding me faintly of something I can't place. Over the last few weeks, I've noticed a lot of teens taking spring jobs before going back to university.

"Yes, thank you." I glance at my watch, fingers tapping

impatiently against my purse while she scans each item at a pace slower than the last.

"Do you need any ice or st—"

"No, thank you. I've got everything I need." I swipe my card, the reader flashing green in approval, then scoop the bags into my arms. "Thanks," I call over my shoulder as I head out the door.

A LITTLE OVER AN HOUR LATER, I pull into the event hall's lot—coffee in one hand, bag and laptop in the other. Later than I intended, but better a little late and caffeinated than never. After waving to the receptionist, I make a beeline down the hall to my office.

The back of the hall is divided into a dozen small offices, each sparsely furnished with a desk and chair. A practical use of space by the owner, renting them out by the week or month. I set my coffee on the desk, sink into the leather chair, and power on my laptop.

My fingers fly across the keyboard, dispatching a dozen emails in quick succession. When I finally glance up at the clock, it reads half past ten. I'm making good progress.

Was Carter making any progress finding the wolf pup?

My cell buzzes, and I grab for it, half-wondering if my thoughts had summoned him. Disappointment twists in my gut when the screen lights up with a reminder to call the decorations store. No new messages.

He doesn't need to text me. He has his own life; I have mine. We're both hardworking, career-driven people. Just because my stomach does summersaults every time he looks at me doesn't mean I need to act like some schoolgirl with her first crush.

Pulling my planner from my purse, I flip to this week, drag out my highlighters, and cross off *emails* from today's date. Next on the list: pick up decorations. Not worry about crazy ex-boyfriends. Not chase tails with handsome wolf shifters. And definitely not mope about *what ifs*.

I am happy. I am successful. And I'm going to throw myself into work—like always.

I hit *call* and put the phone to my ear. It rings once, twice.

"Enchantations Decorations. How can I help you?"

"Hello, this is Rosemary. I placed an order earlier for an upcoming event. I was hoping to check the status? I have the order number."

"Oh yes, I believe your custom decorations have arrived. You can pick them up this afternoon."

I sigh in relief. Getting the decorations early lifts a huge weight off my shoulders—I can start setting up now, since nothing's perishable like the flowers or food.

"Fantastic. Everything came in? The balloon arches, banners, tablecloths, garlands, and branded gift bags?" I tick the items off on my fingers.

"Yes," she replies, followed by the rustle of a box being opened. "What an unusual shade of—" The phone goes silent before she clears her throat. "Chartreuse?"

I sputter, choking on my coffee. Surely I misheard.

"Did you say *chartreuse*? As in the French liquor? As in yellow-green?" I shoot to my feet, pacing the length of my tiny office.

"Yes, miss," she squeaks.

Oh no, no, no. This is not good. The decorations were

supposed to be deep blue—like the sky at dusk, like the ocean in winter. Not split-pea-soup green.

"There must be some mistake. Are you sure those are the decorations for the Wise Fox Lounge's opening? They should be blue."

When I'd met with them in person, I'd pored over the pattern books for what felt like hours until I found the right shade to bring the lounge's vision to life.

The hum of her sigh fills the pause.

"I'm not sure what happened. Your order very clearly states cerulean blue. Do you have another associate who may have called and asked for a color change?"

No one else was leading this project. No one even knew where I was sourcing my supplies.

"No." I slump back into my chair, rubbing my temple. "Please tell me it can be fixed before the event."

"Unfortunately, with your event so soon, I can try, but I can't guarantee the replacements will arrive in time with such a custom order. Did you still want to pick these up? You can return them if the others arrive in time."

"Thank you. I'll stop by tomorrow afternoon."

I set down my phone and bury my face in my hands. It's too late to order from anywhere else. I could piece something together, but nothing would coordinate. If only I specialized in illusions instead of emotions—I could spell them the right color and be done with it.

CHAPTER 10
ROSE

The buildings blur as I drive down the double-lane highway toward the decorations store. Soft pop blares from the radio, but I can't shake this unsettling feeling. I woke up to another note shoved under my door. After Jett and I broke up and he started harassing me, I'd hired a local coven who specialized in protection spells. They placed wards to keep unwanted intruders out, but apparently they don't consider paper from an infuriating ex an intrusion.

And if that wasn't enough, Ginger—being his ornery self—had knocked over the houseplant Netti gave me as a move-in gift. It lay wilted and sallow in a sad pile of dirt when I found it this morning and tried to repot it by the window.

Maybe it's a sign.

"It's not a sign of impending failure," I whisper, gripping the steering wheel. "I am powerful. I am worthy. I am successful."

Despite the odds—and my mother's constant eye-rolls—I

do believe we draw energy to ourselves. And right now, I need all the positive energy I can get.

I exit the freeway and follow the GPS until I park in front of a whitewashed building with a cheerful sign that reads *Enchantations Decorations and More.*

"Maybe the girl on the phone was color-blind?" I mutter as I sling my purse over my shoulder and walk toward the door. A chill slides down my spine, the prickle of eyes burning into the back of my neck. I turn slowly, scanning the street, but nothing seems out of the ordinary.

"Stop worrying so much, Rose," I chide myself, pushing inside. Yes, a long vacation after this would be well deserved— if I manage to pull off this grand opening.

"Welcome to Enchantations Decorations. How can I help you?" A willowy, middle-aged man with a grey handlebar mustache greets me from behind the counter near the door.

"I'm here to pick up an order for Rosemary Sinclaire." I pull the folded paper from my purse and hand it over.

"Ah yes, one moment, miss." He turns and disappears down a row of shelves and through a door into the warehouse.

I take the opportunity to peruse the aisles. Pops of colors in dozens of shades line the shelves, perfectly categorized. Every shade—except blue. The spaces between green and purple are bare.

Completely sold out? That feels like more than bad luck.

The last time I was here, I'd been in too much of a rush to browse. I could lose hours in this shop; it's an event planner's heaven, stocked with everything from baby showers to retirement parties. But with the sour twist of anxiety at every missing shade of blue, I can hardly look at anything else.

The rhythmic click of wheels on tile draws my attention

back to the front, where the clerk pushes a cart stacked high with brown boxes.

"Would you like to double-check the product?"

Do I want to? No. I'd rather avoid the issue entirely, but the sooner I rip this bandaid off, the better.

"Yes, please," I reply, fingers tapping the edge of my purse as he produces a box cutter and slices open the first box. I hold my breath, chanting in my head: *Make it blue, make it blue.*

The air rushes out of me as he folds back the cardboard flaps, and my eyes are assaulted.

Chartreuse. And calling it chartreuse was polite. The color leaned closer to the putrid vomit I'd produced after ignoring my parents' warning and downing an entire gallon of lime sherbet when I was seven. To this day, I avoid lime at all costs.

"It's quite an... interesting shade of balloons," he says before glancing up. "Oh dear, is something wrong?"

My throat tightens, but I shake my head and swallow the bubbling anxiety.

"It's just... not the shade I was expecting. When I called, I was warned there was an issue with my order."

"I see. It does appear as though you ordered cerulean blue. Perhaps it's just the balloon arches."

One box, then another, then another—each one revealing that same nauseating green. My stomach lurches with every cut of the blade.

"We can put in another order and see what we have in stock," he offers.

"I already checked. Outside of baby-shower décor, your blues are gone. Balloons, banners, even tablecloths—sold out."

"That can't be possible. We just got a shipment last week. It may not be the exact shade, but I'm sure we can find something more fitting than"—he glanced over his shoulder, mustache wrinkling in distaste—"that."

With a sigh, I gesture for him to proceed. I trail behind him through the aisles. The lines pulling down the corners of his mouth deepen with every empty bin, box, and shelf we encounter.

"This is most peculiar. I'll have to call the other associates. Perhaps one of them pulled the product to show you?"

"I'd appreciate it," I reply, though I don't let the flicker of hope grow. Who would buy out every shade of blue? Something doesn't add up.

"Do you want us to keep these?" He gestures to the dozen boxes, barely masking his displeasure.

"No, I drove all the way out here. I'd rather have something than nothing in case it doesn't work out." Maybe I could call around and see if anyone was willing to glamour the decorations on short notice. I'd known a witch or two in school who would glamourize their hair color—what were a few decorations?

"If you wish. If you do not use them, we do have a thirty-day return policy. Do you need help out?"

"Thank you, I can manage." I take the cart by the handles and push it toward the door, pausing when my phone begins to ring. The screen lights up with Netti's photo, and I hit *answer*, tucking the phone between my ear and shoulder.

"Rose!" Children squeal in the background, crackling across the speaker, and I can't help but smile as I continue pushing the cart to my car. "I haven't heard from you in forever! How are you? Is now a good time?"

"Anytime is a good time for my best friend." I stop and glance up at the sun sliding past its peak. I'd spent more time in the store than I realized.

"I know it's a ways off, but I also know how busy we both get. Hush, Isabella, go to your grandmother."

I chuckle, leaning against the cart. "I thought you were learning to run the clinic?"

"Well, I am, but I took the afternoon off and got roped into watching some of the pups since it's spring vacation. Which reminds me about vacations..."

I love my best friend—and her quirky, neurospicy brain that could be healing one moment and chasing a new hobby the next.

"Something we both are sorely in need of. What did you have in mind?" I smile, my thoughts drifting back to the lake and forest where I'd surprised Netti with a visit over a year ago.

Where I met Carter for the first—and last—time. That weekend was still wildly vivid in my dreams, still lingering in my thoughts. I couldn't explain the instant attraction I'd felt for that man. Yes, he was drop-dead sexy, but so was his twin—and Connor never made my insides flip the way Carter did with a single glance. Even the way he said my name...

"Rose? Rose?" Netti's voice pulls me back, and I shake my head.

"Sorry, I thought I saw something," I mumble, pushing the cart the last few feet to my car.

"No worries. As I was saying, I heard about a little town up in the Pacific Northwest that's great for holiday getaways. Furnished cabins you can rent. I thought maybe we could do a girls' weekend, just get away like we've always talked about."

"Oh, a cabin trip? That would be great. With cocoa and cookies?"

"That's exactly what I was thinking. A little quiet, a little peace. I know we both could use it."

My brows pinch together, Netti's words fading away as something else catches my eyes. My tires. My *flat* tires.

"Hey, Netti, that sounds great, but I actually need to go. Can I call you back later?"

"Oh, yeah. Just don't be a stranger." Another child starts yelling in the background. "Love ya, girlie."

"You've got it. Love ya more."

I hang up and walk toward my car, abandoning the cart as I circle around it. Not just one, but four flat tires. Four *slashed* tires.

Tears prick at the corners of my eyes. Who would do this?

That's when I see it—the photo tucked into my driver's window. A photo of Carter and me walking down the street, arms full of paper bags from the sandwich shop.

My stomach lurches as I turn it over. Jett's familiar scrawl slices across the back:

Who is this?

Anger boils hot in my chest, mingling with the sting of tears. What did I ever see in him? Why did I try so hard to prove myself?

My teeth grind, hands clenching, and the air crackles with magic until my car alarm erupts, wailing through the lot.

"Crap." I fumble for my keys, hitting the alarm button until the noise dies, the parking lot falling back into the hum of the city.

I glance from my ruined tires to the stack of boxes on the cart. I could call a tow, but I still had errands to run—the florist appointment, then home to feed Ginger. Netti was too far away, my parents were off in Peru, and I wasn't close enough with anyone at my new job to ask for help.

My gaze drops to the photo in my hand.

Carter.

I tap his contact, staring at the little chibi wolf I'd set as his image so I wouldn't have to look at his real face every time I opened the list. A tow truck could get me to the tire shop, but after the day I've had, I could use more than just repairs. I could use a strong, cold drink.

"I shouldn't bother him," I mutter out loud. He's not here leisurely—he's looking for that missing girl. The one I'd volunteered to help find.

But then I glance again—first at my slashed tires, then at the photo of us.

He *did* say to call him if I needed anything.

I hit the button.

The phone rings once. Twice. Three times. My thumb hovers, ready to hang up—

"Hello?" His groggy voice rasps through the speaker.

***

Carter steps off his bike, pulling off his helmet and raking a hand through his short dark hair with a low whistle.

"What did you run over to end up with a flat?" His rough voice does things to my insides I don't have time to think about right now.

"It doesn't matter. Thanks for coming." I wave off his question. He already disliked Jett and acted overly protective of me —the last thing I need is him going full *shifter* if he finds out this was my ex.

"I told you to call me for anything. Even if it's just a flat tire, I couldn't leave you stranded."

"How did you get here so fast?" I ask, attempting to redirect the conversation.

"Lucky for you, I was already in the neighborhood. I was going to check out the club you mentioned. Wait"—his gaze drops to my car, eyes flashing gold before returning to blue—

"is that *four* flat tires?" His voice hardens. "What happened, Rose?"

Damn him and his sharp eyes.

"Nothing. Could you just take me to the florist? They close soon." I bite my lip and gesture down the road. "Plus, I have connections with the club. Easier to get us in to talk with the owners than for you to swagger your way in looking for clues."

"Rose." His voice is a gravelly warning as his hands close around my shoulders, turning me to face him. "One flat is an accident. Four at once?" He releases me, crouches by the tire, and runs a hand over the rubber—right where the jagged slash gives me away. His head lifts slowly, eyes glowing feral gold, a low growl vibrating in his chest. "Who did this?"

"It's probably just some punk kids playing a prank," I lie with a shrug, meeting his gaze. He doesn't buy it for a second.

"Rose." He rises, forcing me to face him eye to eye. "You're the worst liar. It's written all over your face. Who did this to you?"

I sigh and drop my head, resisting the urge to lean into him and spill everything onto his leather jacket. My fists clench around the crumpled photo. His nostrils flare as he notices it, flipping it over to reveal Jett's messy scrawl.

His growl deepens. "This the same ex who left the note at your house?"

"He's harmless. He must've seen us the day I was helping you and got jealous. He doesn't know we are—" My throat tightens. What were we? Not dating. But every second, I wanted him to jump my bones.

"Yes, Rose. What *are* we?" He steps closer, fist crushing the paper at his side. I back up, not trusting myself, until my thighs bump into something cold and metallic. I glance down, and that's when I remember what my so-called knight in shining armor came riding in on.

"Oh no."

"Oh no, what?" His voice is a dark temptation, his breath brushing my neck, sending heat spiraling through me even as apprehension grows in my stomach. My eyes lock on the blue rocket he calls a bike.

"I'm not riding that death trap."

"You mean Elenor?"

"Elenor?" I choke on a laugh, pointing at the glossy machine. "You named your bike Elenor?"

"What's wrong with Elenor?" He pats the leather seat like it's a beloved pet. "She's perfectly safe."

"Safe? Do you know how many people *die* riding those things? I'll call a cab. You can just—" I wave vaguely down the street. "You can go be a superhero for someone else. Rescue another damsel in distress."

"What you mean," he drawls, "is you're not riding it like that." He gestures to my outfit, then unzips his leather jacket in one smooth motion. "And you're not climbing into a cab with a stranger. Not after what happened to your car."

The unsaid words—*after your ex stalked your house, your job, then slashed your tires like a maniac*—hang heavy between us.

"Carter," I protest, though it comes out weak.

His words barely register as my gaze snags on his forearms, muscles roped tight, thick veins standing out as he grips the jacket and holds it out to me.

"Rose?" His voice softens, barely a whisper. I drag my gaze upward, meeting his eyes. "Don't you trust me?"

"We barely know each other. Why should I?" The words leave my mouth, brittle and untrue, even as I slip my arms into the jacket he slides over my shoulders. Warmth envelops me as he zips it shut.

Hurt flashes across his face, gone in an instant, but guilt stabs through me. I shouldn't have said it. If I didn't trust him—even a little—I never would've called.

"I'll never be just a stranger to you," he says quietly, before turning to the bike. He pulls his helmet over his head, then pauses, lifting the more feminine twin from the saddlebag. He holds it for a long moment, visor hiding his expression, before gently sliding it over mine.

CHAPTER 11
CARTER

"Ready, kitten?" I say into the helmet's mic, grateful I'd sprung for the feature. The parking lot is quiet now that the tow truck has gone, only the occasional hum of a car passing on the street.

"To voluntarily get onto that beast?" Her voice crackles through the speaker as she gestures at my bike, its metallic blue surface shimmering like sunlight on the ocean against the dark asphalt.

"If you have a problem riding on top, we can work on that." I smirk, picturing the blush creeping over her cheekbones.

"That's not what I meant, and you know it!" she hisses, posture stiffening.

"I know. Just trying to ease the tension." I rest a hand on her lower back, guiding her toward the bike. "She doesn't bite."

But I do.

I roll my eyes at my wolf's antics, settle onto the seat, and extend a hand.

"I don't know the first thing about riding motorcycles. There isn't even a seatbelt. What if I fall off?" She eyes my hand warily.

"I won't let you fall."

She climbs on behind me, and my wolf rumbles in contentment.

"Where do I—"

"Feet here. Hold on." Her hands slide around my waist, repositioning at my instruction. "Here we go."

The bike rumbles to life, and I ease us onto the main road. As our speed builds, her fists clench against me, heat burning through my thin shirt, a sharp contrast to the wind pelting my skin. Even over the roar of the engine, I hear her heart racing.

"Breathe. I've got you, kitten," I murmur.

"I told you to stop calling me that," she says, though her tone softens and her grip loosens slightly. "So prepared with two helmets. Do you take women for rides often?"

The bite in her voice warms my chest.

"Jealous?" I tease, picking up speed. Her arms cinch tighter around me.

"No. Just wondering how many heads have been in this helmet —and whether I need to treat myself for fleas when I get home."

"Wolf shifters don't catch fleas." I chuckle.

"Fleas, lice—same difference." She pokes me in the ribs.

"Getting brave, kitten. Careful, or you'll let go."

We want her gripping us, needing us.

"I thought you said you wouldn't let me fall," she quips, her arms squeezing in a death grip.

"I won't. But letting go makes my job harder."

Amongst other things.

"Just answer the question, wolfie." She scoffs, sitting stiffly behind me.

Silence settles, heavy as the engine's hum fills the space where words should be. My hands flex around the handlebars, cool night air brushing my neck as I wrestle with how much to give her.

"Carter?" Her voice cuts through, tentative.

"Do you really want to know?" I press the throttle, stretching the moment.

She hesitates—I can feel it. The way she's weighing whether pressing me will push me away. Seconds pass. A minute. The road unwinds endlessly ahead. Neither of us bends.

Then she exhales sharply. "You know what? Forget it. It doesn't matter."

Something in me breaks. "No one." The words rip free before I can stop them, raw and desperate. My chest tightens, the need to give her more clawing at my throat.

The silence that follows shifts—heavier, charged.

Her head tilts, and I imagine her eyes narrowing. "No one?" she echoes, testing my words.

I swallow, forcing myself to remain calm, letting her hear the truth I've never given anyone else. "No one has worn that helmet," I say, voice low and rough. "And no one has ever ridden my bike. Ever."

Except you.

The words hang, bare and undeniable, louder than the engine, louder than the rush of wind.

"Oh." Her reply is soft but heavy, and I feel the weight of a hundred unasked questions between us. If only I could read her mind. If only she could feel my emotions. Why was I the only one she couldn't read?

WE DRIVE the rest of the way in silence until we pull up in front of Flouramor Florist. The shop is a cheerful, quaint brick building tucked between a row of small storefronts, its tall glass windows painted with crisp white letters spelling out the name, framed by curling vines and floral sketches. Bouquets as big as armfuls block the view inside. We circle down the alley and into a parking spot. Sliding off, I hold out a hand to help Rose off the bike.

"So?" I ask, setting my helmet on the seat and raising an eyebrow.

"So what?" she says, pulling hers free. The breeze ruffles her dark auburn hair, and my pulse races at her scent.

Mine.

I clear my throat and smirk, jerking a thumb at my bike.

"Did you die?"

"You're such an asshole." She shoves the helmet into my chest and stomps around me, but I catch her the wrist, tugging her back until we're chest to chest. I lean down, close enough our noses nearly touch.

"What was that?" I whisper, breathing in her intoxicating scent.

"I—" Her tongue darts out to wet her bottom lip. I let go of her wrist and cup her cheek, her heartbeat thrumming against my palm.

She wants us. Look how she melts at our touch. Does she feel the pull of the bond the way we do?

"Rose." I drag my thumb across her plush lip, her mouth parting under the touch.

What are you waiting for? Kiss her.

Her phone buzzes, and she jumps back, cheeks flushed and chest heaving. She fumbles through her purse, pulls out her phone, and paces the length of the brick wall. A few minutes later, she thanks whoever was on the line and puts the phone away.

"Everything okay?" I ask, noting the smudges under her eyes, the slump of her shoulders. I want nothing more than to pull her into my arms, to kiss her senseless and ease some of the weight she carries. But I know her—she thrives on staying busy, on helping others. As an empath and conduit witch, her magic and heart are wired that way. Still, she shouldn't have to do it alone.

"Yeah. Just the band I booked for the Wise Fox Lounge opening canceled." She rubs her temples and groans. "First the decorations, now this. I want this to go perfectly. I *need* it to go well."

What you need is—

"Tsk, tsk. Buckle up, buttercup." I tip her chin up, tucking a strand of hair behind her ear before straightening the collar of my jacket.

"Oh! Your jacket." She reaches for the zipper, but I cover her hands with mine.

"It looks good on you. Besides, we've got a few more stops before I can whisk this princess home—before the clock strikes midnight and my trusty bike turns back into a pumpkin." I tap her nose and step away.

Rose shakes her head, but her smile carries a little of that lost sparkle. "Last I checked, wolf shifters weren't fairy godmothers. And I'm not headed to a ball."

No, but I could play prince charming—and I wouldn't need to try a shoe on every maiden to find you.

"You're a brilliant witch and damn fine event planner from what I hear. Where one door closes, another opens. This might not be a ball, but as long as I'm in town, I'm at your service. Now, let's go smell the roses." I give a mock bow and offer my arm. She chuckles, takes it, and together we step into the florist.

Two hours later, after slogging through catalogs of flowers, vases, and goddess only knows what else, Rose finally meets me in the lobby. I'd spent the time reaching out to Alexandria's family, hoping for news. Nothing solid—just a message to her friend confirming she was still in town.

"Ready?" I ask, handing her the helmet.

"Yes. Summerwind is just a few miles down the street." She fits the helmet on after giving me directions, then climbs behind me without her usual fuss. We take off. Having her pressed against me feels so damn right, and it's all I can do not to pull over, drag her into my arms, and show her everything I've held back—the things I've thought about every night for the past year. Watching from a distance. Waiting.

But we're done waiting. We won't let her slip away again—not when we can still feel how she reacts to our touch.

"Turn here," she says, and I roll into the nightclub's parking lot. A line already snakes around the building, the setting sun painting the sky in streaks of fire.

Heads turn as I park and Rose swings off the bike, tugging off her helmet and shaking free her hair. In the evening light, she practically glows.

"That's a long line." I whistle low, scanning faces, hoping for a glimpse of the wolf pup. It would be too easy is she were standing right there, but I wouldn't complain.

"We won't need to wait. I know the owners and almost all the staff." She nods toward the bouncer checking IDs at the door. "Ready?"

"Well, isn't that lucky?" I follow her to the front of the line, ignoring the heated glances aimed at my mate.

"Hey, George. Busy night?" The tall, broad male turns, grin splitting wide as he pulls Rose into a hug, then holds her at arm's length.

The bass thrums through the walls before we even step inside, vibrations settling low in my chest like a second heartbeat. Neon light spills from under the door, pulsing with the rhythm of the music. The faint tang of alcohol and sweat lingers in the air.

"Rosemary Sinclaire. Aren't you a sight for sore eyes?" George tsks, his sharp eyes sweeping her from head to toe. "Though it looks like you've been working yourself to the bone again."

Rose arches a brow but only smiles.

George shifts his gaze to me, grin turning sly. "And who's this fine wolf shifter on your arm?"

"This is Carter," Rose answers easily. "We're looking for a girl—hoping we might find some luck here."

George's smile falters. "Now, Rose. You know I'd do anything to help, but—"

Before he can finish, I pull my phone from my pocket and flash the picture. Rose's voice sharpens, cutting through the bass. "It's a missing girl. One of the wolf pups, nearly ready for her transition, has run away. We've had word she's in town. Have you seen her?"

George studies the photo, lips pressing together. Regret flickers across his face. "Sorry. Can't say I have. I've been off the last two nights. But I'll keep an eye out." He glances over his shoulder, then pushes the door open. A wash of sound spills out. "If I were you, I'd ask the owners."

As Rose tugs me forward, I lean close. "Let me guess—you know the owner?"

"Owners," she corrects with a grin. "I've booked bands for them before."

The club swallows us whole. The pounding beat vibrates up through sticky floors, colorful lights flashing over the crowd. Onstage, a four-piece band thrashes through a punk anthem, the audience shouting lyrics like a war cry.

Rose points toward the bar. "There."

Three willowy figures stand out even in the chaos, golden hair cascading like sunlight, their brown skin glowing under the shifting neon. The crowd parts around them without thought.

"Fae?" I murmur.

"Wood nymphs," Rose replies, her grin bright in the shadows. "Triplets—rare, brilliant, and beautiful."

She pulls me toward them, weaving through the crush of bodies, the beat pounding in time with my pulse.

"Rosemary, what an unexpected surprise." One embraces her, plucking at her windblown hair. "The elements look good on you, witchling. Where have you been hiding?"

"Not hiding. Just working." Rose tucks her hair back, and I fight the urge to run my fingers through it.

"And what brings you to visit, with such delectable company?" Their chocolate eyes flick toward me in unison.

"Erythena, Elayna, Ellasia—this is Carter." Rose fidgets with her purse strap.

"Welcome to Summerwind, Carter." One drags a delicate finger down my arm, and Rose stiffens beside me.

"Thank you." I nod politely, gaze scanning the room instead.

"I'm going to say hi to Sapphire and get us drinks while you talk with them," Rose says, gesturing to the red-haired bartender before slipping away into the crowd.

Carter, don't let her out of our sight.

Her scent still clings to me—stubborn, sweet—but it's drowned by sweat, booze, fae magic, and the sharp bite of vampire musk. My wolf bristles. I track Rose weaving through bodies with a confidence that screams this is her world, not mine. My fingers twitch with the urge to follow, to keep her close, but I force myself to stay put. This is her territory. I'd only get in the way.

"Wolf shifter," one of the triplets purrs, "what do you think?"

The nymph slides into my space before I can exhale, her hand gliding up my arm and curling against my chest like she has every right to touch me. My jaw tightens. The fae's contact sparks nothing. Hollow. Mechanical. Empty. Not like when Rose is close. When she looks at me, I feel seen. When she speaks, I feel as though she's pulling me apart piece by piece— and somehow, I want her to.

"Of the club?" I ask, twisting slightly to break her touch. I'd heard fae were physical creatures, that they often communicated through touch. But there's only one woman I want touching me, and she's currently walking away to gather clues about the missing teen.

My eyes flick to the stage, then sweep the chaos of the dance floor—anywhere but Rose. "Can't say I'm much for nightclubs. But... the music's decent."

"Yes." She frowns, though her gaze follows mine. It doesn't take long for her to spot where it lands—on Rose, laughing at something Sapphire just said, her smile brighter than any of the club's neon.

"Are you with the witch?" she presses.

"Rose?" Her name tastes too familiar on my tongue, and I know it shows. Heat crawls up my neck as I stumble over my answer. "I'm actually here on business. Rose was hoping you might be able to help us."

"Such a shame," the other two sisters say in unison, dancing wantonly to the beat and gesturing pointedly at me. "We'd love to help you."

"Fabulous," I mutter, ignoring their obvious advances as I pull out my phone. "Have you seen this girl?"

They pause and lean in, lips pressed together.

"Yes," the first says at last. "She was here last night with a fake ID—so close to eighteen, and so pretty for a wolf shifter."

My pulse spikes. "What did you do?"

"We called her a cab and sent her off, of course. We may run a nightclub, but we have morals when it comes to children."

"Do you know where—"

"No, thank you. I'm not interested." Rose's voice cuts through the bass and crowd. I snap my head toward her. Two vampires are coaxing her onto the dance floor, her bartender friend nowhere in sight.

Don't touch what's mine.

I storm forward without thinking, slipping an arm around her waist. My canines elongate as I growl at the vampires.

"I believe the lady said no," I snarl. "I suggest you listen. She may not bite—but I do."

"There's no fighting allowed in the club," one protests. "We only wanted one little dance."

"There are also rules against forcing patrons against their will," the triplets intone in unison as they appear beside us, the air crackling with unseen earth magic. "If you wish to continue visiting our property, you'll abide by them."

The vampires scatter, and the triplets turn to us.

"Unfortunately, your little wolf pup didn't tell us where she was going. We just made sure she left here safely. We will, however, keep an eye out and alert Rose if we see her again."

"Thank you. I hope all has been well," Rose says, leaning into my touch. Instinctively, I tighten my arm around her waist —a silent promise of protection.

Good job, Captain America.

"Yes, thanks to you," the triplets reply. "If there's any way we can repay you, we're indebted for the success you've brought to our club more times than we can count. This won't be the last you see of us." Their voices carry a cryptic edge, a vow lingering in the air. Then, as one, they melt seamlessly back into the crowd.

Rose exhales softly, relief and exhaustion bleeding into the sound.

I pull her closer until the warmth of her body presses into mine. "Let's get you home, sleeping beauty," I murmur, low and intimate, my lips brushing the shell of her ear. She leans into me, light against my chest, and I guide her through the throng toward the exit—unwilling to let anyone, or anything, come between us tonight.

CHAPTER 12
ROSE

A knock at the front door wakes me, and I grope for my phone, wondering who would be here this early. Carter and I had driven home late last night in comfortable silence. Despite his teasing all day, he hadn't made any advances when he dropped me off. Part of me had been disappointed as he turned away, my fingers brushing unconsciously against my lips.

The knock comes again, louder this time. Groaning, I roll out of bed, tug on my robe, and shuffle toward the kitchen. Ginger mewls at my feet.

"Not now," I say through a yawn. I was not a morning person, and staying out late had only made it worse. Not to mention, I'd been in the middle of a steamy dream about the wolf shifter haunting my every thought. The very shifter I had no business thinking about—not when I had work to do, and he had a mission for his clan.

The knocking grows more insistent. I haven't missed any

calls, so what could it be? This had better be an emergency, or I was going to hex whoever dared interrupt the best sleep I've had in months.

"I'm coming!" I grumble, padding to the door. Peeking through the eyepiece, I spot Carter's bike parked in the driveway, his familiar silhouette turned away.

"Carter? What are you doing here? Is everything okay?" I ask as I crack the door open—only for Ginger to dart out between my legs.

"Good morning, Ro—what was that?" Carter spins, arms full of bags, the smell of bacon and coffee curling in the air.

"Hold on!" I sprint past him, feet hitting the cold cement as I chase Ginger around his bike. "Come here. No, leave his bike alone!" Ginger finally trots up to Carter and rubs against his pant leg, purring.

"I'm so sorry," I pant, holding out my arms. "He never runs out like that."

"Seems your kitty likes me," Carter says, smirking as Ginger curls on his shiny black shoes.

"I thought cats and dogs didn't get along," I snipe back, scooping him up. "What are you doing here?"

"Touché, kitten." He lifts the bags. "Since I kept you out late, I thought I'd bring breakfast."

"Oh, you didn't have to do that. You're the one who rescued me. I owed you." My stomach betrays me with an audible growl.

"Have and want are two different things." He shifts his weight. "May I come in?"

I eye him, then the offering. I could never resist food. Touch and emotions might be my magic, but food has always been my love language.

"Yes," I concede, stepping past him into the kitchen and

setting Ginger on the floor. "It's not like you're a vampire barred from entering without permission."

Carter chuckles, setting the bags on the counter. From one, he pulls out a drink carrier with two steaming cups and hands me one. I gratefully accept and take a long swallow of the sweet caramel macchiato.

"No, that's just a fable. But I wouldn't barge in without permission. Besides, I could sense the wards around your house."

"They're meant to deter ill intent, though they're not infallible."

And clearly doesn't apply to objects from individuals with ill intent.

"Also, wolf shifters can detect magic? I didn't know that." Across the counter, Carter pulls two warm breakfast sandwiches wrapped in brown paper from the bag.

"Let me grab some plates," I say, stretching for a pair from the shelf. But as I step back, my foot lands on Ginger's toy. I slip, plates wobbling—until Carter's arms close around me, warm and solid, pulling me against his chest. His breath is hot at my ear, my skin burning through my clothes where we touch.

"There's a lot you don't know about me, kitten," he murmurs as he steadies me and sets the plates on the counter.

"Yes, well. Thank you for breakfast." My cheeks burn as I tuck my hair back and take a plate.

We eat in silence, comfortable yet charged.

"Rosemary? About last night..."

Heat pricks my eyes, jealousy sharp in my gut. I have no reason to feel this way—he's free to see whoever he wants.

"It's not my business if you want a... thing with those fae," I mutter, staring at my empty plate. "The triplets have a reputation for their taste in shifters."

Carter chokes on his coffee, pounding a fist against his chest as he stares at me, dumbfounded—his eyes flashing gold before settling back to cerulean. "What are you talking about?"

I swallow hard, the memory of the triplets' lingering stares twisting in my stomach. "I saw the way they were looking at you. Right up until the vampires started harassing me. You didn't have to come to my rescue. I could've handled it." I shove my plate into the sink. "Thanks for breakfast. I'm sure you've got other places to be."

"Rosemary." His voice drops low, commanding, and I freeze as he steps closer, bracing his hands on either side of me against the sink. My pulse pounds, the heat radiating off him nearly unbearable. "I have no interest in any of the owners of Summerwind. Let alone all three of them."

My chest tightens, breath catching as his gaze locks on mine. It's raw, claiming, as if I'm staring straight into his wolf.

"I wouldn't blame you if you did," I whisper, the words slipping out before I can stop them. My fingers curl against the edge of the counter. "Anyway... I shouldn't waste more of your time. I need to get to work."

I try to duck under his arms, but the robe I'd tied loosely comes undone, revealing the soft blue silk of my pajamas clinging to my curves. Heat floods my cheeks as I fumble to close it. Carter's lips twitch into a dangerous smirk as his golden eyes rake over me, drinking me in.

"Work can wait," he growls, voice low and feral, his hand brushing my hip. "Tell me, Rose. How do you plan on getting there?" He shifts to lean casually against the counter, the sun streaming across his profile, gilding his tanned skin and unruly hair. Adonis himself, standing in my kitchen.

"I—" And then I remember why I'd stayed out so late in the first place. My tires. I close my eyes and groan, rubbing my brow. "Shit, my car."

"Don't worry. I called the tire shop this morning. Your car's ready to pick up, and I can drop you off whenever you're ready." He glances at the watch on his wrist, then casually sips his coffee.

Goddess damn this man and his impeccable thoughtfulness.

AFTER CARTER DROPS me at the tire shop, I head straight to my office. Thanks to the slashed tires and yesterday's disaster at the decoration store, I'm now a day behind on my duties at the event hall—and the grand opening. The boxes still need to be dropped at the lounge, though the last thing I want is for Angelique to see the wrong color and send me packing. Somehow, I also have to find a replacement band before opening night.

I sigh, push open the door, and make a beeline for my office, pausing only long enough to wave at the receptionist. The hall hums with voices and the steady clatter of keyboards from every office I pass, and I pray no one stops me.

At my desk, I sink into the chair and pull out a pad for a new a to-do list, setting my coffee on the moon-shaped coaster Netti gave me last Christmas.

The moon. Carter.

As if I needed another reminder of the wolf shifter who won't leave my thoughts—or the weekend we spent together, which somehow feels like both an eternity ago and only yesterday.

Was he affected as much as I was? Does he ever regret not taking things further, not pushing when I insisted long distance wouldn't work with my schooling and job?

I shake my head to clear my wandering thoughts and refocus on my office. A stack of letters waits on my desk—mostly invitations to openings, band tours, and private parties from places I'd helped with during internships. I flip through them for anything urgent before setting them aside, then pull out my laptop and calendar, turning to the monthly page. With careful strokes, I cross off today's date.

Seven days until the grand opening of the Wise Fox, and I still had a mess to untangle. At least the macarons were safe—I'd phoned the bakery on my way back, and they assured me the order would be ready the day before.

"Macarons and flowers down. Let's see about the rest."

I tap the end of my pen against the desk, resisting the old habit of chewing caps—a nervous tic I'd dropped years ago after Netti's horror stories, though the urge still lurks whenever deadlines tighten.

"Who could cast a glamour strong enough to hold over every decoration?" I mutter, scrolling through my contacts. Nothing. A few witches might manage a centerpiece or two, but enough to keep the whole lounge from flashing puke-green mid-opening? The last thing I needed was the Wise Fox turning into a split-pea nightmare at the stroke of midnight.

"Rose, have you met Dria?" Susan's voice carries from the hallway. I push back from my desk, stretching stiff muscles. The receptionist appears in my doorway with a teenager in tow—dark wavy hair with golden highlights piled into a messy bun, rich olive skin glowing under the fluorescent light.

"She interviewed yesterday," Susan explains. "She'll shadow me at the front tomorrow."

I freeze, studying the girl. Déjà vu prickles sharp down my spine.

"Do I know you?" I circle my desk and extend a hand. The moment our palms meet, my magic flares. A flood of emotions slams into me—excitement, fear, awe, apprehension. I send a pulse of calm, watching her shoulders ease before I let go.

"I'm sorry, ma'am. I don't think so," she says softly, bowing her head.

"She's been at the local grocer for a few weeks but wanted a change," Susan adds with a laugh. "Says she's interested in travel and event planning—remind you of anyone? Perhaps you could take her along for a day. Just don't scare her off with stories of overworking."

"Where did you say you moved from?" I fold my arms over my chest, studying Dria closer. Faces stick with me, voices too —even after years. And hers sparks something I can't quite place.

"Oh, my family's from a small town—you wouldn't know it. I moved here to get some experience and, well, you know." She laughs nervously, rocking back on her heels.

"Yes, I'm well aware of how family can be, small town or not." I smile, hoping to ease some of her nervous energy.

"Actually, speaking of family, I should head home. I told them I'd only be gone an hour for the tour."

"Alright, see you tomorrow—" But she's already turning, her footsteps echoing down the hall.

"Youth," Susan says with a shrug.

"Do you think she'll be a good fit?" I watch Dria's retreating form, still nagged by the sense I've seen her before. "She seems anxious. Flighty."

Both qualities I can't handle right now—not with the

lounge's opening only a week away. What I need is stability and calm, not another variable I can't control.

"We'll see how tomorrow goes," Susan replies as we both stare at the door swinging shut at the end of the hall.

CHAPTER 13
CARTER

She's been here. I can smell her.

"I know, but it doesn't look like she's here anymore. Her tracks stop cold right outside the store," I grumble, pacing the grocery aisles, shading my eyes against the too-bright overhead lights. I hadn't slept all night, patrolling outside Rose's house with the scent of her ex fresh on the doors and windows. She said the place was warded, but I wasn't taking chances. Not after that stunt he pulled yesterday.

We should bite his head off for even thinking of our Rosemary. She's ours.

"We don't have time to go hunting." Yet. If he tried anything else, I wasn't holding back.

What we need is—

"If you're about to say what I think you are, keep it to yourself. Rose needs time."

She needs us. She wants us. You're a fool to ignore how she responds to our touch.

"I'm very aware. But in case you've forgotten, we're here to find a missing wolf pup. So start thinking with your head, not—"

Find the girl, send her back to the pack, then pursue our mate. Roger that.

"That's not what I meant, and you know it." I stare at the photo of Alexandria until my vision blurs. After seeing Rose safely to work, I'd gone back to the hotel and managed a fitful nap. Nights on guard duty and days full of micronaps were wearing thin. "Where are you?"

Carter.

The tug at my core pulses, but I shove it down and scroll through my messages again, checking for clues I might've missed.

Carter.

"I know—we need food, sleep, and her. But first we need answers." I probably look like an idiot, standing here in front of a wall of chips staring at my phone.

"Carter?" A warm hand brushes my forearm. I glance up into ocean blue-green eyes. Rosemary's eyes.

"Rose? What are you doing here?" My brows furrow, and I flick my wrist out of habit to check the time, even though every screen in the world now shouts the hour. "Shouldn't you be at work?"

"It's half-past five. I stopped for groceries. Is everything alright? You look like a zombie."

"Half-past five," I echo, rubbing a hand over my face. How long had I been standing here dazed? "Zombies don't exist..."

Her lips twitch. "Witches, werewolves, and vampires exist —but you draw the line at zombies?"

"Have you ever seen one outside a movie?"

"No. But just because I haven't doesn't mean they're not

real." She eyes my basket. "So why are you here? Can't decide between extra cheese or salt and vinegar?"

"I just... lost track of time. Tracked the girl's scent to this store, but it went cold again." I flash her the newest photo of Alexandria in a bright yellow sundress.

"Wait. I've seen that dress." She bites her bottom lip, tapping her foot.

"On the girl?"

"No—on a mannequin. Recently. Somewhere in town." She leans close, zooming in on the photo, her scent wrapping around me until my wolf hums. "But I can't recall which store."

"How many clothing shops are in this town?" I mutter, resisting the urge to nuzzle her temple.

"Well, there's Alfred's on 39th, Elise's Boutique, Fernando's..." She ticks off names on her fingers.

"Okay, there's a lot—I get it. But I don't have time to hit every store."

"Well, maybe we could tag-team?"

"Neither of us can waste a whole day wandering stores. What we need is a lead." My thumb hovers over my brother's contact before I accidentally hit *call*.

She's hinting she wants time with us, idiot.

I glance up, catching the flicker of disappointment in her face before she masks it with a forced smile. The phone rings. Too late.

"Carter, good to hear from you. Any luck?" Connor's voice cuts through the line.

Rose turns away, her basket swinging at her side as she studies the wall of chips.

"That's why I'm calling. The trail's gone cold—"

"You know what can happen—"

"I know," I snap, dragging a hand through my hair.

"You never call for help," he says dryly. "You're such a stubborn ass, you must really need it. What's the magic word?"

"I don't have time for games," I growl, my eyes fixed on Rose watching me from the corner of her eye.

"Nope. Don't recall those being it. Try again."

"Connor, this isn't the time—"

"How's the witch?" His smirk all but crackles through the speaker. He's spent the last year needling me to move on, while I buried myself in work. Anything to forget that weekend. Anything but her.

"Fine. Please."

"Send me what you've got. Good luck." The line clicks off without so much as a goodbye. I forward the photos, updates, and a note for him to dig into Rose's ex.

Purely for her safety. Not because we want to rip him to pieces.

"Any luck?" Rose asks.

"Connor's on it. Though I doubt he'll find more than I have."

"Hopefully he does. I worry about her, and I don't even know her." She slumps, gaze dropping.

"You worry about everyone, kitten." I tip her chin up, her soft skin stark against my rough calluses. "You give too much, feel too deep, and never expect anything in return."

And you love too hard.

She holds my gaze, her tongue flicking over her bottom lip.

Tell her about the bond. Mark her. Make her ours.

"Rose—"

"What are your plans for dinner? Looked like rain on my drive over."

"Dinner?"

"Yes, dinner. That meal you eat in the evening? Don't tell

me werewolves skip it. How else do you grow so big, strong, and handsome?" She pinches my bicep.

"You think I'm big, strong, and handsome?" I lean in, caging her against the shelf.

"That's... ah." Her pupils blow wide, pulse fluttering at her throat. "I was just teasing."

"About inviting me to dinner—or my size?" I lift a brow, savoring the way she squirms.

She ducks under my arm and points down the aisle. "I'm no chef, but this place has the best freezer lasagna. And blueberry cheesecake."

An hour later, we're sitting across from each other in her living room, Ginger purring at my feet.

"You weren't kidding. If I didn't know better, I'd think you'd made that lasagna from scratch."

"Well, adding extra cheese on top helps," she says, blushing as she gathers the plates and sets them in the sink.

"Here, let me. You did the hard work of cooking." I take the sponge and quickly wash the dishes, stacking them neatly in the drying rack.

"You don't have to do that."

"Of course I do. I may be a guest, but cleaning up after myself is the least I can do. Besides, if I didn't clean up at my place, I'd be overrun with strays." I chuckle, scratching Ginger's head. The little furball closes his eyes and purrs louder. I don't usually like cats, but he's growing on me.

You're laying it on a little heavy. Just kiss her already.

"What are your plans once you find the girl?" Rose asks.

I straighten, meeting her gaze. "I'm not quite sure."

"What do you mean you're not sure?"

"Well... I was thinking about traveling. My duty to the clan has lightened significantly."

Her hand stills over the kettle on the stove. "Travel sounds like fun. Ouch!" She jerks back, jamming her finger into her mouth.

"What happened?" I'm at her side in a heartbeat.

"It's nothing. I just brushed the kettle," she mumbles around her finger.

"Come here. Cold water helps," I murmur, taking her wrist. I lift her hand and inspect the reddened tip. "Doesn't look too—"

My mouth goes dry. Beneath her usual berry-and-cream scent lingers another: wolf shifter. I bring her wrist closer, inhaling.

"Carter." She giggles, tugging against my hold. "That tickles."

"You found her."

I drop her hand and spin her around the small kitchen, too elated to stop myself.

"What?" she says breathlessly, bracing her palms on my forearm when I set her down.

"I thought I smelled her earlier when I ran into you, but dismissed it as a lingering trace. It's stronger now. She's been near you."

"The girl?" Her jaw drops, then she slaps her forehead, cursing as she clips the injured finger.

"Here." I grab an ice cube from the freezer, wrap it in a paper towel, and cradle her hand between mine. "You need to be more careful."

"You don't need to keep rescuing me."

"I'll always be here for you."

Thunder cracks outside, rattling the windowpanes. Rose jumps, glancing at the front door.

"It's just a storm," I reassure her. "Don't tell me you're afraid of a little thunder?"

"No, I'm not afraid." She crosses her arms and purses her lips, but her eyes keep darting toward the glass.

"What are you afraid of?" I tuck a stray strand of hair behind her ear.

"N-nothing." She turns briskly to the stove. "Tea?"

"Why don't you sit down? I'll check the perimeter before the rain hits." I guide her gently toward the couch. "Then we'll talk about why you smell like a dog."

"I do not smell like—" She whirls, eyes wide, cheeks blazing pink as she sniffs at her blouse.

"Relax. I was joking. Well, about *you* personally smelling like a dog. You smell incredible as always. But there's another scent clinging to you," I say.

"Then what are you talking about?" Her brows knit. "It's not very nice to tell someone they smell and then leave them hanging."

"Sit tight. I'll explain in a moment." I give her shoulders a reassuring squeeze. She scowls but sinks onto the couch, waving me toward the door.

Outside, the sky's gone a deep, storm-bruised maroon. I shift, dropping onto all fours, power humming through my limbs as my wolf takes over. The neighbors might panic at a giant wolf prowling the block, but with the storm rolling in, most are tucked safe inside.

I circle the house quickly, but nothing seems amiss. No fresh trace of her ex, no disturbances beyond the steady rumble of the storm rolling in.

Then I the round the corner—and the sky splits open. Rain pelts down in sheets, drenching my fur in seconds.

Great.

"Carter?" Rose's voice drifts into the night, soft and sweet, pulling me back. She stands framed in the doorway, kitchen light at her back, a silhouette of beauty against the storm.

Silent on padded feet, I prowl toward her. She startles, hand flying to her chest until her gaze sharpens on me.

"What are you doing? You're soaking wet—get inside," she hisses, pulling the door wider.

I brush past her, water dripping onto the tile from my fur.

"Why are you in your wolven form? Did you find something?" she asks, twisting the hem of her shirt between her fingers. Ginger pads out of the living room, sniffs the humid air, then prances back as his paw splashes in the cold puddle forming on the tile.

Rose extends her hand, and I lift my elongated snout to her wrist, inhaling deeply. Young female wolf shifter. It had to be her. I will my body to shift back, magical reserves draining at the sudden double change. I'll need to load up on protein soon.

"Sorry. My senses are sharper as a wolf, especially my ability to sense magic," I explain, swiping wet hair out of my eyes. "And I can move faster."

"Stop skirting around the subject and just tell me what's going on." She plants her hands on her hips, eyes sparking, and it takes everything in me not to grab her sassy little frame and kiss her senseless.

"Why don't *you* start by telling me why you smell like a wolf shifter?" I shoot back.

Her brow furrows. "Wolf shifter?" She doesn't blink, staring me straight in the eye.

"Yes." I step closer, lowering my voice "A *female* shifter, in particular."

Her gaze finally breaks, dropping to the floor as her toe scuffs against the tile. "I didn't want to say anything until I was sure, but... they interviewed a new girl to train at the event center."

"And you didn't think to tell me?" The words come out sharper than I intend, but the thought of her keeping this from me claws at my chest.

"I didn't want to get your hopes up!" she snaps, chin lifting defiantly. But it cuts more than soothes.

"You can't just keep things from me, Rose," I growl, pacing a step away. Water drips down my temple, my clothes plastered to me, heavy and cold. I rake a rough hand through my soaked hair.

When I spin back toward her, chest heaving, she's... staring.

Mouth parted. Eyes wide. Like she's forgotten what we're arguing about entirely.

"What?" I demand, glancing down at myself. Nothing's out of place—except that I'm standing in her kitchen, drenched, shirt plastered to every muscle, jeans leaving little to the imagination.

"Rose?" I tilt my head, trying to read her.

She clears her throat, gaze darting anywhere but my chest.

"I—uh—I didn't mean to lose my temper," I say quietly, trying to ease the tension. "Maybe I should go back to the hotel."

"No!" The word bursts out of her before I can take a step. She presses a hand flat against my chest, and fire races through my veins at the contact.

My wolf strains forward, demanding more.

"You're soaking wet," she murmurs, softer now, all the fight gone from her voice. "It's pouring outside. You'll get sick if you stay like this."

"I'll be fine," I reply, though my voice roughens when her hand lingers. "I've endured worse."

"I didn't mean to hide what I found out today from you," she says. "I don't want to argue with you, Carter. Not over this. Not when we…"

Thunder cracks and she flinches, eyes flicking to the window again. Her lips press together, thoughtful, before she gestures vaguely at me from head to toe.

"I don't want to fight either. I understand your reasoning, even if I don't agree with it." I tuck a stray strand of hair behind her ear that had fallen loose from her bun. "I'll stay—but only if you want me to. First, I need to get out of these wet clothes, so I don't drip all over your house."

"I don't exactly have clothes that would fit you," she admits, cheeks flushing. Her gaze lingers a second too long over the outline of my torso. I nearly smirk, realizing my wet jeans leave nothing hidden. "But… you could wrap up in one of my oversized bath towels while your clothes dry in the dryer."

Bath towels. She's seen you in less.

"Works for me." I shrug, peeling the wet cotton shirt over my head, fully aware of the show I'm giving her.

She swallows, voice low, her eyes never leaving my chest. "And maybe… we could watch a movie."

"I'd like that," I murmur, squeezing her small hand in mine.

Which is how I end up with my mate curled against my bare chest, a storm raging outside, her breathing slow and

My pulse spikes with rage. How many ways did I have to show him I wanted *nothing* to do with him?

I slam the flowers into the trash. The card follows, crushed in my fist before I bury it under the wilted stems.

Flowers. If he'd ever listened, he'd know I hate them. I'd told him a dozen times—watching them wilt, watching them die, scraped at something raw inside me. Wasteful. Pointless.

But that was Jett in a nutshell, wasn't it? Tone-deaf. Self-absorbed. Always giving me the exact thing I never wanted and acting like it was a gift.

I glare down at the trash, chest heaving. He thinks he can win me back with flowers that will last as long as his promises of faithfulness?

Pathetic.

I hate cut flowers.

I push through the lobby doors and scan the reception area, but Susan and her new apprentice are nowhere in sight. I need to find them. Need to know if this girl is the one from Carter's clan so he can finally settle his mission.

But then what? Would he walk away, back to the clan—leaving me behind, as I once left him after that first weekend?

Did I even want that?

"Susan?" My voice echoes faintly as I head down the hall toward my office. Half the rooms I pass are unoccupied. Not unusual on a Friday—most renters like an early start to the weekend—but it feels emptier than usual.

"Down here," Susan calls. Following the sound, I find her and the new girl rummaging through the supply cabinet. Susan glances up from her clipboard, her face brightening.

"Morning, Rose. You look glowy today. I wasn't expecting you for another hour or two—you usually come in later on Fridays."

I force a smile, hoping she can't hear the frantic pace of my heart. "Thanks, Sue. I skipped the coffee shop and came straight in. I've got a long list of things to tackle. You know how fast summer goes by and then all the fall and winter events around the corner." I nod toward the girl, grateful for the excuse. "If you don't mind, I'll take over showing her around. The front always needs extra hands before the weekend."

Susan arches a brow. "That would be fantastic, but are you sure? With everything going on at the Wise Fox, you must be swamped."

"I'm positive." The words come a little too quickly, but I can't let her see the knot in my stomach every time I think about the lounge opening in less than a week. The Wise Fox feels like a dream balanced on a knife's edge—one wrong move and it all comes crashing down. I force a wider smile, feigning calm I don't feel. "Besides, the Wise Fox can't interfere with my job here. This comes first."

Unless, of course, the lounge opens a door I can't turn down. Wasn't that the dream from the start? To travel, to keep moving, to never be tied down? The same excuse I once gave Carter when I pushed him away.

Susan's shoulders ease, her relief obvious. She never did like training—too set in her routines. "Well, if you need anything, you know where to find me." With a small wave, she heads back toward her desk.

I turn to the girl, inhaling slowly to steady myself. How would she react if she knew the truth about me? Could she smell Carter on me as clearly as he had scented her?

It wasn't so long ago I was her age, straddling that impossible line between teen and adult—straining against rules that felt suffocating while craving freedoms I wasn't ready for. Back then, all I wanted was adventure. Now, with the weight of secrets pressing on my chest and a business teetering on the edge of its grand opening, all I want is simplicity. Rules. A little certainty in the chaos. And maybe the stability of a certain wolf shifter by my side.

I square my shoulders and offer her what I hope is a reassuring smile.

"Rosemary, isn't it?" She crosses her arms and eyes me warily.

Did she sense my magic the last time we met? Did she know what I was—and who I suspected she was?

"Yes. Rosemary Sinclaire. I've only recently started here as lead event coordinator, but I've traveled all over the world during my college years and internships." Her brows lift, her posture easing.

Good. I've piqued her interest.

I glance over my shoulder, but Susan is nowhere in sight. That doesn't mean she won't return at any moment. What we need is privacy. Susan didn't know I was a witch—and she certainly didn't know about Dria. Many humans were aware of the supernatural's existence, but I could only handle shocking so many people in one day.

I slide my foot back, nudge the door shut, and the overhead light hums softly, dim yellow against walls stacked high with boxes of supplies and decorations.

"Now, Alexandria—" I begin, but the girl freezes. Her eyes dart between me and the closed door like a deer trapped by a wolf.

If only she knew I'm more of a fat house cat at heart—content with cream and a warm windowsill.

"How do you know my name?" she demands, a flicker of golden flashing in her brown eyes, her body tightening like a bowstring.

"I—" How was I supposed to explain who I was? Or mention the tall Alpha wolf currently tracking her down without sounding like an overbearing parent? "I was a teenager once too. Wanting freedom. Wanting travel."

"Look, I don't know who you think I am, but I'm just here for a job." She moves to brush past me, but I shoot out an arm, catching hers. I draw on my magic—her emotions flood into me in a chaotic rush, and beneath them, something else stirs. A wild animal, prowling under her skin.

Shit.

I don't know much about adolescent wolves, but between Netti and Carter, I've heard enough to know I don't want to be around when one loses control.

"Let me pass," she whispers. Her voice is low, rough, and her hands clench at her sides, nails lengthening into dark claws. Her irises spark, molten gold bleeding into brown.

Great. Rose, you've managed to piss off the hormonal teenager and trap yourself in a tiny closet with her. Brilliant. Netti used to compare her younger brother to a zombie when he was a teen—this was closer to a rabid beast. A literal one.

I raise my other hand, but Alexandria seizes my wrist, claws pricking my skin.

"Alexandria, I'm not here to hurt you." I send a flood of calming magic into her, drawing on every happy moment I can muster. Netti and I giggling through our first sleepover. Buying my first car with my own money. Opening my acceptance letter to the school of my dreams. Last night, falling asleep against Carter's side.

"Move," she warns, claws biting deeper. "I don't want to hurt you, but I will if I have to." Some of her fight wavers though, stuttering against my magic.

"Dria, I'm not here to tell you what to do or drag you back to the pack," I say, gently loosening my hold and stepping back until my spine brushes the door.

"You're... not?" Her shoulders dip, claws retracting, golden flecks in her irises dimming until only brown remains.

"No." I let out a slow breath. "But I do have answers. More than we can hash out in a closet." My lips twitch into what I hope is a reassuring smile. "And do you know what I think? That I need the rest of today off. And some more coffee." I flick the latch behind me. "Would you like to come?"

I hold my breath, hoping she accepts the olive branch. As an only child, my experience with kids was limited to Netti and her brothers—and none of them had ever sprouted claws on me.

She studies my face warily, then flicks her gaze toward the hallway before returning to me.

"But what about my training? I really need this job." Her hands curl into fists at her sides. "You don't understand. I need—"

"Part of this job is assisting," I cut in gently, unwilling to let her slip away. "You'll be assisting me. I'll teach you what you need to know after I answer your questions."

Her lips press together, then she blurts, "Do they have food there? I didn't realize how expensive food was." A flush creeps into her cheeks.

Relief loosens the knot in my chest. I swing the door open and gesture for her to follow.

"Of course. I'll take you to one of my favorite places to eat." I smile and lead the way toward my office. "We can go over everything—this job, what it entails—while we're there."

Half an hour later, we're settled in my favorite spot by the window, the table between us piled high with plates covering nearly half the menu.

"So you really traveled overseas to intern at the Corpse Flower Gala?" Dria's eyes go wide as she devours half her BLT in a single bite.

"Slow down—you'll make yourself sick. Have you eaten at all today?" My gaze flicks to her plate, already littered with crumbs, and the other half of her sandwich still clutched in her hand. "Dria?"

She shrugs, avoiding my gaze. "I've had a few things here and there since moving here, but all the money I brought ran out fast. That's why I need this job so badly." Her big brown eyes lift to mine, pleading, and my heart softens. "I didn't realize food and travel would cost so much. I'm not even paying rent yet."

I reach across the table and squeeze her hand. "You'll get there. But you don't have to do this alone."

To answer her earlier question, I add, "Yes, that was one of the most fascinating events I ever had the chance to work on as an intern. The costumes were... otherworldly." The memory brings a smile to my face, the chaos and glamour of that whirlwind week still vivid.

"What did you wear?" she asks, polishing off her sandwich before gulping down her iced mocha.

"Well, I found this tiny boutique a couple days before the gala. It cost almost all my savings, but—"

"She wore the most stunning silk gown—midnight blue, studded with tiny gemstones, enchanted to drift like a cloud around her. She was the night sky itself. People couldn't stop staring. Rosemary was the talk of the gala, featured in tabloids for weeks afterward."

Carter's voice rumbles behind me. He steps up, hands gripping the back of Alexandria's chair.

The color drains from the girl's face. She looks like she might hurl the entire contents of her stomach onto the table.

"Carter?" My brows knit as I tilt my head toward him. "How could you know that? I don't recall you being there."

"I wasn't," he admits easily, pulling over a chair from a nearby table. His gaze lingers on me, burning, before he sits and leans back. "But I would've paid good money to see it myself. Netti showed us."

Heat flares up my neck under his stare.

"You told him I was here?" Dria hisses, snapping her accusing eyes to me. She shoves her plate away, pushing back as though ready to bolt. "I thought you said you weren't sending me back to the pack."

Carter tenses at her words, every muscle coiled, but I lift my hand, silently telling him to wait.

"I didn't ask him to meet us here to drag you back to the pack." I take a slow sip of my latte, letting the warmth steady me before I continue. "I brought him because, as much as I know about magic—and being a teenage girl—I don't know what it's like to be a teenage wolf."

"I *have* control over my wolf," Dria snaps, eyes glowing gold, a low growl threading her voice.

"Do you?" Carter cuts in, his gaze sharp. He nods toward the table, where her claws are extended, carving shallow grooves into the wood. "It takes *years* to master that kind of control."

He falls silent for a beat, face flickering with something—pain, regret, memory—and I wonder what he endured at her age.

"What Carter means," I say gently, leaning toward Dria, "is that we're not here to punish you. We want to help. I see your passion and your dreams. But I also know how dangerous uncontrolled magic can be."

Her gaze swings back to me, fierce and pleading all at once. "I don't want to go back. I've made friends here. I have a job."

"A job?" Carter arches a brow, his tone skeptical.

"They hired her to help part-time at the event hall," I explain quickly before she can bristle further. Then I turn back to Dria. "But part-time isn't enough to sustain living on your own."

"And your parents *are* worried," Carter adds, leaning forward, forearms braced on his knees, his gaze steady on her.

"All my parents want to do is control me," she growls, pushing up from the table and storming out of the café.

"Fuck." Carter tosses a few bills on the table, and we rush after her—but she's nowhere to be seen.

"Where could she have gone?" I pant, chasing after Carter, his strides twice as long as mine.

"This way. I can smell her wolf." He turns his head, and for a heartbeat his eyes glow gold.

"Alexandria!" We round a corner into a narrow alley filled with overstuffed garbage cans, the putrid stench of sewer assaulting us.

"I can't smell anything over this," Carter snarls, slamming his fist into a garbage can.

"Wait." I lay a hand on his arm, then push past him, scanning the shadows. At last, I spot her—curled up against the dirty brick wall, tears streaming down her face. I crouch beside her. "Dria."

"Go away," she sniffles, swiping the back of her hand across her face, smearing dirt and tears over her olive skin.

"Let me at least take you where you're staying so you can get cleaned up." I offer her my hand and wait.

"There's no point." She sighs, head drooping.

"There's always a point. And you always have a choice. Great cities weren't built in a day—persistence and determination can get you through anything."

Carter stands silently behind me, the low hum of air conditioners and rush of passing cars filling the alley. Sweat trails down my spine, sticky beneath my blouse, but a little discomfort is worth not rushing her.

"You can't take me anywhere because... there's nowhere to go." She tilts her face toward the sky.

"Where have you been staying?" I ask gently, ignoring the prickling burn in my legs from crouching.

"Here, there." She gestures vaguely, and relief washes through me when her claws retract to her normal nails, painted electric purple and neatly rounded. "I've met a few friends. Mostly witches, a couple shifters, even a fae. I've crashed at their places sometimes, but mostly I've been staying at the park in my wolf form at night. I didn't realize being on my own would be so hard. I thought I could move, find a job, get my own place, do my own thing."

"Life is hard," I say softly, "but it isn't impossible."

Her eyes finally meet mine, and I smile as she slips her hand into mine. I help her to her feet.

"You can come back to my place tonight."

CHAPTER 15
CARTER

Three hours later, after a trip to the department store and grabbing takeout pizza, Rose and I stand in her kitchen sipping cans of soda while Dria watches TV in the living room.

"I should get going. It's getting late," I say, tipping back my can and glancing at the darkening sky beyond the window, streetlamps flickering on in golden halos.

Or we could stay. We're already planning to sleep outside.

"And leave me here alone with a teenage werewolf?" Rose laughs, eyes crinkling as she shakes her head. "No way. You got me into this mess."

"Leave you? You're the one who charmed her. I'm just in the way." I crush my empty can in one hand, drop it in the recycling, then gather up the paper plates and pizza box.

"You're not in the way," she says softly, twisting a lock of hair around her finger, gaze fixed on the can in her other hand. "I've enjoyed your company. Even if it did almost get me mauled."

"From what I recall, *you* voluntarily locked yourself in a broom closet and then accosted a teenage wolf shifter who's highly emotional and volatile." A smirk tugs at my mouth. If only I'd been there to diffuse the situation—but thankfully, the witch had been quick on her feet and even quicker with her magic.

Our witch.

"When you put it that way." A loud snore drifts from the living room, and we both glance at the teen sprawled on the couch, the television murmuring in the background. "It was a pretty rash decision on my part."

"It was a very bad idea." I step closer, needing to be near her, needing to brush against her.

Mine.

Her breath hitches, and she looks up at me, nodding before whispering, "Yes, a very bad idea."

I could think of some other bad ideas we could try.

"Why did you do it? You knew you were putting yourself in danger." My gaze drops to her wrist, where a faint bruise and scratches mar her skin—marks I hadn't noticed in the bustle of the afternoon. The hairs on the back of my neck rise, my jaw tightening until my teeth ache. "She hurt you."

Fuck, my voice is too deep, too rough. I'm on a razer's edge —every instinct screaming to shift, to protect my mate—logic slipping further out of reach.

"Carter, it's okay. No need to go all wolfie on me." She lifts her wrist slightly, dismissing it with a small shake of her head. "It was an accident. I put myself there knowing exactly what I was dealing with. She was just... afraid."

I lightly brush her wrist and step back, staring at the claws sharpened to lethal points at the tips of my fingers. I'd never lost control like this before.

Rose was fine. It was an accident.

"Carter?" She steps forward just as Ginger darts between us. She stumbles, her soda can flying from her hand and dousing us in sticky brown liquid before she collides with my chest.

She tilts her head back and bursts out laughing, her cream shirt plastered to her skin. Every nerve in my body ignites, fire beneath the cold spill, as I stare down at her.

Kitty deserves an extra treat for that.

"Shh," I murmur into her hair, tightening my arms around her while my gaze flicks to the still-sleeping form on the couch. "You don't want to know what happens if you wake a sleeping wolf."

"Is that so?" Her brow arches as she looks over her shoulder, then back up at me, eyes dancing. "Well, we'd better get cleaned up before we risk disturbing her."

I scoop her into my arms, her muffled giggles vibrating against my chest as I carry her into the other room. Setting her gently on the cool bathroom tile, I reach around her in the close space, push open the glass shower door, and twist the knob.

"I'll just go clean up," I say, turning toward the door—but Rose's warm hand lands on my arm. I stop, meeting her gaze as she turns me back.

"Thank you," she whispers, her eyes bright with something more than happiness—lust. She rises on her toes and presses a soft kiss to my cheek, her lips lingering. I inhale her sweet berry-and-cream scent, my hands finding her waist almost instinctively.

We stand there for what feels like an eternity, suspended in a moment neither of us dares break.

"Carter," she says quietly, almost sheepish before her gaze lifts boldly to mine. "There's room for two."

It's all the permission I need. I pull her against me, one hand sliding up beneath her shirt to the small of her back, the other curling into the hair at the nape of her neck as I claim her sweet lips with mine. Her lashes flutter shut, mouth parting, and it takes everything I have not to consume her here and now on the bathroom floor. She deserves more than a hurried romp on cold tile, and I won't risk scaring her away.

I break the kiss, both of us breathless, my forehead resting against hers as I hold her close, her heartbeat hammering against my chest. The tug inside me tightens, undeniable.

"That was—" she begins, voice trembling, but I silence her with another kiss, sealing her to me, branding her into my very soul.

"Hush, let's get you clean. Hands up." My voice comes out gruff as I grip the hem of her shirt. She obeys instantly, lifting her arms so I can tug the soaked cotton over her head and toss it aside. The silk bra beneath clings to her curves, each breath drawing my eyes lower, slower.

My palms trail down her sides, savoring every dip and rise until I reach her waist. Dropping to one knee, I ease her pants down. She steadies herself with her hands on my shoulders, her skin flushed, body trembling as I free her from the damp fabric.

The steam builds, filling the bathroom with warmth, wrapping us in it. Her blush deepens as I look up at her, soda-slick hair falling into my eyes.

"You're not getting in the shower fully clothed, are you?" she teases, tugging at the neck of my shirt.

Instead of answering, I press a kiss to the inside of her

thigh. Her breath catches, a soft moan slipping free as her fingers dig into my shoulders, eyelids fluttering shut.

"No," I murmur against her skin, letting a wolfish grin tug at my lips, "but I'm not done helping you." I trail slow kisses higher, my hands sliding up the backs of her thighs to cup her smooth, rounded bottom. Nuzzling against the cool satin of her panties, I draw a gasp from her lips as her knees buckle slightly beneath her.

"Carter," she moans as I hook my fingers under the elastic band, pulling them down to reveal smooth, bare skin.

"*Fuck*, I love how you say my name," I whisper against her center, burying my head between her thighs. She melts under my touch like molten chocolate to a flame, her head thudding back against the bathroom wall.

"I want..." I nip at her inner thigh, and she gasps, legs trembling as she squeezes them together. I lift one over my shoulder for better access, admiring her spread before me—my own personal dessert.

I want you.

"More?" I pull back, and she whimpers.

"Please."

"As you wish." I feast on my little witch as she moans, her fingers scraping along my scalp. She's so close—I can smell her arousal, feel her body tensing. It's better than I ever dreamed in all these months apart. "Goddess, I love the way you taste. The way you smell."

"Carter, I'm close," she whimpers, and I'm more than happy to oblige, sliding a finger inside her.

"Take what you need," I growl against her sensitive flesh as she rocks her hips. I slip a second finger in, my dick straining hard against my jeans.

Her back arches as she moans, clenching around my

fingers. The air vibrates with magic, bottles and accessories floating before crashing back down onto the counter.

"Carter, that was—" I silence her with a kiss as I stand, deftly reaching behind to unsnap her bra. Turning her toward the shower, I give her bare ass a tap.

Torture. Now take her and give her what she really needs. Mark her as ours so everyone knows.

"Time to clean up." I strip off my shirt, admiring the fresh scratch marks across my shoulders. She steps into the shower, eyes glossy with lust and satisfaction as she watches me.

I make quick work of my jeans and follow her in. She reaches for me, but I catch her wrists in my hands. "Not tonight."

"But—" Her brows furrow as her gaze drops, but I ignore the protest, reaching past her for the loofah and soap.

"It's been a long day, and tomorrow will be even longer, figuring out what to do with the girl." I run the loofah over her smooth, pale skin, brushing her long hair aside as I wash her from neck to toe. My hands follow after, massaging her muscles, lingering over her calves and back.

"You're right." She sighs, leaning her head back against me, her spine pressed to my chest as my soapy hand slides across her breast and pinches her nipple lightly. She gasps, and I nip at her neck without breaking the skin as my other hand slips between her thighs.

"But perhaps you deserve one more, for being such a good girl," I whisper against the shell of her ear. I slide two fingers inside her, pumping leisurely as I caress one breast, then the other. My dick is rock hard, pressed between us, but I ignore its throbbing.

"Carter," she pants, her hips rocking as I quicken my pace, my free hand gliding up to gently encircle the front of her throat. I tip her head back against my shoulder until her body tenses and release overtakes her. She turns, and I trace my thumb along her bottom lip, her tongue darting out to taste her arousal before I hungrily claim her mouth, pressing her against the shower wall.

We break apart, and I make quick work of rinsing down while she catches her breath, her eyes never leaving me.

I turn off the water, and we both dry off before heading into the bedroom—when I remember Alexandria asleep on the couch.

Fuck. The whole reason we were pulled back together in the first place is this mission. I only hope our ruckus hasn't woken her—or worse, scared her off. The last thing I need is to explain to her parents how we found her and then lost her.

"I'll see you in the morning?" I ask, scooping up my clothes from the floor.

"You're not going out in sticky, soda-soaked clothes in the middle of the night," she says, one hand on her hip.

"Last I checked, I didn't bring a change of clothes—and you already have one houseguest." I gesture toward the closed bedroom door.

"Last *I checked*, we're both consenting adults, and I have a king-size bed. Plus, you already said tomorrow's going to be a long day. Go throw your clothes in the washer and come to bed. I promise to behave." She points down the hall.

What if I promise not to behave?

"Rosemary..." I protest, though my resolve is slipping fast. It's one thing to make her feel good and then spend the night outside guarding her. It's an entirely different test of will to lie beside her in bed. Either way, I'm not planning on getting much sleep.

She drops her towel with a shrug and walks away—her ass,

a perfect curve that could give the moon a run for its money, swaying as she bends to pull a cream silk nightdress from the dresser and slips it over her head.

Why that little witch.

She crawls under the covers on the right side of the bed, patting the empty space beside her with a smirk. "I thought you were a wolf, not a chicken."

She's going to be the death of me.

CHAPTER 16
ROSE

The smell of bacon wakes me, the sizzle and pop from the frying pan echoing through the kitchen. I glance at my phone as I push off the covers, startled to see the digital clock reading almost ten a.m.

When was the last time I slept in this late?

Grabbing my robe from its hook on the back of the door, I pad into the kitchen to find Alexandria at the table, shoveling forkfuls of pancakes into her mouth. My stomach growls at the scent of syrup and bacon.

"Good morning, kitten," Carter says, waving from the stove. He's wearing the bright pink apron Netti gave me two years ago—the one that reads *Don't trust skinny chefs* across the front. "How do you want your eggs cooked?"

"Eggs?" I glance at the stovetop and counter where a half-empty carton of eggs sits open beside a plate piled high with pancakes. "What are you doing?"

"Cooking breakfast. What does it look like?" He waves a

pair of rubber-tipped tongs in the air, splattering bacon grease on the floor. Ginger licks it up greedily before purring and rubbing against Carter's legs.

Is he trying to win everyone over?

"Yeah, but what are you doing *cooking* in my kitchen? Where did all this even come from?" I gesture to the half-empty jug of orange juice on the counter.

"Well, I went to the grocery store," he says matter-of-factly, flipping the bacon without breaking eye contact.

"You went shopping for food *and* made breakfast—all while I was sleeping?" I arch a brow, eyeing the two of them. They glance at each other, then back at me, like guilty children. "What's the catch?"

"No catch. I just know how ravenous teens can be—especially teen wolves." He shrugs, turning another strip of bacon before nodding toward the carton of eggs. "And after looking at your nearly empty fridge, I figured you wouldn't want to deal with that first thing in the morning. Oh, and I grabbed you coffee from the café. It was on my way back."

I take the proffered cup, pop off the lid, and drink deeply—sweet caramel macchiato, just the way I like it.

"Eggs?" he asks again, setting another pan on the stove and lifting the carton.

"Over easy. Now tell me your motive." I level him with a look over the rim of my cup, eyebrow arched, channeling my best undeceived attitude. "Why go through all this trouble instead of just picking something up?"

"Okay, fine." He glances over his shoulder, but Dria is too busy shoveling food into her mouth with one hand and texting with the other to notice. "Cooking is how I clear my head. I need your help talking her into going back to the pack. She wants to stay here, but it's too dangerous—at least for another year or two, until she learns to control her wolf and goes off to college. Even then, there are procedures."

"Look at her. Do you really think she's going to cause that much harm?" I gesture toward the half-empty syrup bottle and docile teenager, too absorbed in her phone to care about us.

"She needs to go home. She's safer with the pack. She's only a pup." His lips flatten into a thin line.

"She's seventeen, nearly eighteen, in her last year of high school. She's smart, passionate, and has already survived this long on her own before we found her. With some guidance, she can make it outside the pack." I tilt my head in challenge.

"You're suddenly an expert in wolf-shifter upbringing?" He mirrors my expression.

"Did you both forget that even as a teenager I have exceptional hearing as a wolf shifter?" The clatter of silverware on porcelain cuts through the kitchen. We both turn toward Alexandria, who stares at us from the table, her plate empty, phone facedown. Her eyes blaze with conviction. "I don't want to go back. I won't go back."

"Alexandria, we've already been through this—three times just this morning. You need the pack," Carter growls at my side, his knuckles whitening around the tongs as he stares blindly at the bacon, smoke curling up from the pan and filling the air with the scent of burnt meat.

"Give me that." I set down my coffee, snatch the tongs from him, and move the bacon to a plate before shutting off the stove. "No one is going to the pack today."

"I'm not?" Dria perks up, her eyes wide with hope.

"She's not?" Carter turns to me, bewildered.

"Not today at least. She's here under my roof—my protection." I plant my hands on my hips. I was not arguing about this. Not before I'd eaten, and definitely not before I'd finished my coffee.

"Rose, she's part of the pack. You don't understand—"

"I may not know what it's like to be a teen wolf, Carter, but I *do* know what it's like to be a teen with dreams. To feel trapped by family, by magic." My hands cut through the air. "It wasn't easy leaving my coven to pursue my degree and a career that's taken me around the globe. And now? I have a good relationship with my family—but yes, I had to learn the hard way. Dria doesn't have to."

"And what if she goes feral? What if she loses control of her wolf and hurts someone?" Pain laces his voice, tugging at something deep in my chest. I rest a hand on his arm, wishing I could show him what I feel—calm him with my magic.

Why wasn't he affected like everyone else?

"Dria is welcome to stay here until we figure out what to do. She's got clothes, food, and a roof over her head. She can ride to work with me, and the pack already knows where she is." I cross my arms over my chest and wait for his response.

Carter glances between me and Alexandria before throwing his hands in the air. "Connor's not going to like this. It's dangerous. Ultimately, the decision is up to him and the girl's family."

"The *girl* has a name," Dria says, setting her dirty plate in the sink.

Carter turns back to me, raising his brows as if to say, *Are you sure you want to deal with this attitude?*

"It may be the weekend, but I still have a laundry list of things to finish before opening night in exactly..." I lift my hand and count on my fingers. "Six days. So why don't the two of you make yourselves useful—call Alexandria's parents, let them know she's safe, and keep busy until lunchtime. I've got a phone call to make."

AN HOUR later I'm fed, caffeinated, and dressed. The lingering scent of bacon and coffee still clings to my house, and for once it feels like a home. I sit down at the little desk in my room and pick up my phone to video call Netti.

"Rose! Took you long enough to call me back," Netti says breathlessly as she answers.

"Is now a good time?" I drum my fingers on the wooden surface and stare out the window at the flowers blooming in the neighbor's yard.

"Of course. I was just doing some spring cleaning." She sighs and flops down on the couch, reclining in her usual way with her ankles crossed over the chair's arm, her bright pink hair spilling down the cushion. "You look particularly glowing."

"Perhaps you need your vision checked." I chuckle, running a hand through my tangled hair. Ginger hops into my lap and stares at the screen, purring. "I'm a hot mess—overworked, under-slept, and I've spent the last week chasing down runaway pups."

"I may not be able to read emotions, but you look better than you have in months," Netti remarks. "I also hear Carter found the girl—and that you had some help in it."

The corners of my lips tug up as I think about the way he looked at me over dinner last night.

"You could say that," I reply.

"I also heard she's refusing to come home to the pack," Netti says.

"That's actually why I'm calling…" I glance up, nibbling my lip. I've known Netti my entire life—she knows everything about me. Well, nearly everything. How can I tell her about Carter if I can't even be honest with myself?

"Rosemary…" The look she gives me has me wilting in my chair. When was the last time she used my full name?

"I've sensed her intentions and feelings—"

"Rose, I know you want to help every stray you meet, but the things I've learned about shifters since moving in with the pack…"

"Don't you remember what it felt like when we were her age? It wasn't that long ago we were pushing back against our parents' wants and desires for us."

"We also weren't teen wolves whose feral animal side could take over at the drop of a hat. The worst danger we faced was exploding a cup or levitating an object into a window— not mauling a man to death."

My gaze drops to the already fading bruises on my wrist. The girl hadn't even known her own strength.

"There has to be something we can do to help her. How long does this last?"

"I'm not sure." Netti falls silent, her face unreadable as she studies me through the screen.

"She doesn't want to go back. I have a feeling even if we brought her kicking and screaming, she'd just run away again." And this time she'd work harder not to be found.

"You have a point," Netti says with a sigh.

"Between my empathetic conduit powers and your healing ability, there has to be a way to nullify or reduce her wolf's instinct until she can learn to control it." I walk from my room to the kitchen, pull open my laptop, and start jotting down questions to ask Carter when they get back.

"There's something about being around the pack that helps the pups remain calm," Netti explains, and an idea sparks.

"There's something about a witch pursuing her passion that helps stabilize her magic," I counter matter-of-factly. We both know exactly what I mean—we lived it when we left for college.

"And, as usual, you sound like you have a plan." Netti straightens on her couch, leaning forward with her elbows braced on her knees. "I'm listening."

"Well, you've been saying you need a change of pace—and that you miss your best friend in the whole world. Why don't we propose she finish the last two months of school down with the pack? Then she can spend weekends shadowing me, seeing if this is the kind of career she wants to pursue. If it works out, she could intern with me over the summer. We could make regular trips down to the pack. It'd be a win-win, because I'd get to see you more often."

"That's a lot of responsibility to take on. What about freedom and traveling the world?"

I think about how I felt this morning, waking up to Carter in my kitchen making breakfast. Maybe settling in one spot for a little while wouldn't be so bad. Maybe—if he was amenable—we could see if this thing between us could work out.

"I'm really enjoying this new position at the event hall. It might be the change of pace I need."

"Just make sure you're not biting off more than you can chew. Speaking of, how is the lounge opening going?" She leans back, curling up on the couch.

"The lounge? Oh, you know... the usual." I wave my hand in the air for emphasis.

"The usual? What mischief is afoot? The Rosemary I know

is full of confidence when it comes to event planning." Netti raises an eyebrow as she peers at me through the screen, but my gut twists as though she's only a few feet away, wearing that *I told you so, do as I say, not as I do* air about her.

"You're one to talk," I retort. "You jump straight from graduating into a full-time healing position *and* helping with pack responsibilities."

"Idle hands lead to mischief, and you know I always do better when I'm busy." She shrugs, then adds, "But you're deflecting. What's going on?"

Running a hand through my hair, I twist it up into a messy bun and jab a pen through to hold it in place before finally forcing myself to face the glowing screen. My reflection stares back faintly in the glass—tired eyes, lips pressed together in frustration. I exhale through my nose and sink back against the counter.

"It's just... fine, you're right." I rub the back of my neck, shoulders tense. "I may have bitten off more than I can chew, and to make matters worse, nothing seems to be going right. The decorations I ordered weeks ago? Wrong color. Completely useless. And the band I booked canceled on me last minute, so now I've been scrambling to find a replacement."

I drag my palms over my face, muffling a groan.

"On top of helping chase down errant teen wolves and working your full-time job." Her voice crackles through the speaker, too calm for the chaos in my chest. "You need a break, Rose, before you burn yourself out."

"I know." My laugh is brittle, humorless. "And I plan on it. Remember? I told you I'll be visiting the pack more with Alexandria—and you—once this gig is over and the event hall slows down for the summer." I push my laptop slightly away and lean on the edge of the island, fiddling with a stray ribbon from the sample decorations. "Plus, my contract's up for renewal in a couple months. I've got time to decide if I want to stay... or pursue something different."

The words hang heavy in the quiet. My fingers tighten around the ribbon until it leaves a crease in my palm.

Maybe something different isn't such a bad thing. New town. New job. A clean slate, far away from the last messy remnants of Jett lingering in the corners of my life. But would that just be running away again?

I glance at the screen, at the woman who knows me better than anyone. My chest tightens. And then there's Carter—whatever this thing is between us, fragile and fierce, blooming in the space between stolen glances and half-swallowed words.

Would leaving mean losing that too?

"And there isn't perhaps any other undisclosed reason why you'd suddenly be willing to visit the pack so frequently? It wouldn't happen to do with a tall, dark, and handsome—"

"Who is she calling handsome? She better not be talking about Connor. I can't stand being around them making googly eyes at each other more than I have to." Carter's voice cuts in as he pushes open the door, arms ladened with luggage, Dria trailing behind him.

Goddess damn shifters and their impeccable hearing.

"I've got to go, Netti. I'll let you know." I hang up and turn back to the two wolf shifters standing in my living room. My eyes zero in on the luggage in his hands. "What is that?"

"Well, this is the luggage for Alexandria's new clothes from yesterday, along with some toiletries. This bag is my duffel and laptop I grabbed from the hotel when I checked out." He sets everything on the floor and looks expectantly at me.

My stomach plummets, and I fight to keep the disappointment off my face.

Of course. I should've known he'd be heading back to the pack as soon as his mission was over.

Checked out. Out of the hotel—and soon, maybe, out of my life.

My chest squeezes at the thought, but I push it away. There would be time to deal with my so-called love life later. One—no, two—mind-blowing orgasms in the shower did not make a relationship.

"Rose?"

"Sorry, I got lost in thought about the lounge's opening night." I shake my head and turn back to the sink, putting away dishes from breakfast—anything to keep my hands busy and my mind from spiraling.

"How did the conversation with Netti go?" he asks, stepping up behind me, one large hand sliding over mine just as I reach for another cup.

"It went..." I glance over my shoulder and immediately regret it. His cerulean eyes lock on mine, and a tug deep in my core answers, magic humming in my veins, heat pooling low. All I can think about is how he felt between my thighs last night.

"Yes?" He flashes me a wolfish grin, and my cheeks burn. I clap my hands together, duck under his arm, and fix my gaze firmly on Alexandria, refusing to let him see me unravel.

"So, I've got a plan."

CHAPTER 17
CARTER

"I don't like this plan," Connor growls, his arm wrapped around Netti's waist as they stand in Rose's living room. The late-afternoon sun filters through the curtains across her cream loveseat and matching recliner. With three wolves and two witches crammed inside, the place feels overcrowded, and I'm more than ready to have my witch to myself.

For once, we agree on something.

Connor glances at me, and I throw my hands up, the corner of my mouth twitching. "You should know as well as I do that controlling a witch once she's made up her mind is nearly impossible."

My twin chuckles darkly, eyes glinting as he looks down at the petite, pink-haired witch at his side.

"Hey," Netti protests, though the smile tugging at her lips gives her away. She turns toward Rose, who stands in the kitchen, hip propped against the laminate counter.

There are far better ways I'd like to put that counter to use.

"Do I have to?" Alexandria whines, throwing herself onto the couch and covering her eyes with a fluffy yellow pillow. "I don't want to go back. What about my job?"

"I already told you—after you graduate in two months, the internship will be waiting for you. And it won't just be covering the front reception, but shadowing me," Rose says as she pushes off the counter and grabs the handle of Dria's new black suitcase. We'd had to help her repack after she left clothes strewn across the room while trying to decide what to wear today.

"I don't see why I can't just stay here. What are two months really going to teach me?" Dria growls, sitting up, eyes flashing gold.

Easy there, pup. You're in a room with two full-grown wolves and their mates. One wrong move, and going home will be the least of your problems.

A loud rip cuts the air, and the room goes still as we all turn to look at Alexandria.

"What you need to learn is how to control your wolf so you don't hurt yourself—or anyone else—when that happens." A muscle ticks in Connor's jaw as he crosses his arms and nods toward the claws tearing into the yellow throw pillow in her lap.

"Oh." She glances down, then tucks her hands under her arms, guilt written across her face as she looks up at Rose. "I'm sorry."

"It's fine. It's just a pillow. I don't even like the color. I was thinking this summer, when you come up, we could redecorate this place." Rose smiles and pats her shoulder.

My heart warms at the gesture. I watch as Dria's features soften under the soothing wash of Rose's magic, impressed as always by my witch.

Mine.

"Really?" Dria's eyes light up as she jumps from the couch and wraps Rose in a bear hug, her voice muffled against her shirt. "Thank you."

"Alright, time to get going," Connor grumbles, glancing at his watch before taking the luggage from Rose. He always carried a strict air, especially since stepping into his role as Alpha—though beneath it not much had changed.

"Are you sure you can't stay for dinner? There's a great Italian place in town," Rose says, hugging Netti tightly. "It's a little fancy, but the food is to die for."

"I wish. But even leaving now, we won't get home before ten. I promise I'll be back for your grand opening. Connor already promised to take a couple days off to come celebrate with us." Rose glances up at him, and my brother tries to appear disinterested, but I can tell he's never been happier. "Besides, I'd be turned away at the door looking like this."

"Netti, you look like a million bucks. No one would dare turn you away," Rose chides.

"I promise—not today—but we'll be back before you know it." Netti squeezes Rose in a final hug before stepping back beside my brother.

"I'm holding you to your word about coming back up. I thought after we both graduated last year we'd see each other more, not less." Rose wraps her arms around her torso, shoulders slumping.

"I know how much this event means to you. I wouldn't miss it," Netti murmurs, then turns to the teen sulking on the couch. "Come on, let's get the car packed and hit the road."

"Why can't I ride back with Carter?" Dria looks at me with pleading puppy eyes.

"On his motorcycle?" Rose's brows shoot up, her cheeks

flushing as she flashes me a sidelong glance. "Absolutely not. Motorcycles are dangerous."

"But *you* rode on it," Dria whines.

"You did?" Connor and Netti say in unison, first looking at her, then at me.

"Only because he gave me no other choice," Rose hisses, glaring at me—but her eyes betray the mock anger. "I was perfectly happy calling a cab."

"I wasn't going to let you ride with a stranger after your ex slashed your tires."

"What?" Netti exclaims, whipping her head toward Rose. "You never told me this. What's been going on?"

"It's not that big of a deal," Rose mutters, pinching the bridge of her nose. "Besides, don't you guys need to get going?"

It won't be a big deal once I get my claws in that asshole and shred him to pieces.

"Do you need me to send—" Connor starts.

"No," I growl, stepping toward Rose. "I'm staying in town until the opening. I'll be helping her with the decorating."

"You are?" My brother shoots me a questioning glance. "I never knew you to be a decorator."

"There's a lot about me you don't know." I bite my tongue as soon as the words leave my mouth. We're still working on mending our relationship after the years he spent away from the pack.

He just had to go there, didn't he?

My wolf prowls restlessly under my skin.

"You really don't have to," Rose says quietly, resting a hand on my forearm. "I can handle this on my own."

"Actually, I do. I promised to assist if you helped me find the girl, remember?" I can't stop the grin tugging at the corner of my lips as Rose shuffles on her feet, clearly searching for a way out. Joke's on her. After the way she'd responded to my touch the other night—proof enough her feelings for me hadn't changed—I was ready to do whatever it took to win her over, even if it meant crawling on my knees.

"Is it time to go yet?" Dria whines, and we all turn to her—then burst out laughing, the tension in the room breaking at last.

"What happened to not wanting to leave?" Rose chuckles as we walk the three of them to the front door.

"Well, if I can't stay and I can't ride with Carter, we might as well get this over with instead of talking the day away," she says over her shoulder as she heads toward Connor and Netti's grey SUV parked at the curb.

"Text me when you get home," Rose says, giving Netti one more hug goodbye.

"I promise. And you owe me a phone call to fill me in on exactly what's been going on lately," Netti replies, lips pressed together as she glances at Rose, then at me. "And you." She points a finger at my chest. "You'd better take care of my best friend, or I'll curse your next birthday cake."

"She's in good paws." I smirk over my shoulder, which earns me a punch. I feign hurt, rubbing the spot. "Ouch. Careful there, kitten."

"I told you not to call me that," she hisses, her face pinching adorably as she scowls.

"Play nice, kids," Netti says before turning, her pink hair twirling as she jumps into the passenger seat.

Connor circles around to the driver's side of the SUV, and I fall into step behind him.

"Connor, wait." I press a hand against the door before he can grab the handle. Through the tinted glass, I glimpse Rose and Netti still locked in animated goodbyes, while Alexandria scrolls on her phone in the backseat.

Connor exhales, crossing his arms over his chest, weight shifting onto his heels. "Yes?"

"Do you remember Alexander—the one who used to play bass guitar?" My mind flicks back to the wolf shifter we'd known years ago, the one who'd ditched pack life to tour with his band while I stayed behind to take on Alpha duties. We'd lost touch after that.

Connor squints at me. "Yeah, I remember. Why?" His gaze keeps darting to the car, restless.

"Do you still keep in contact with him?"

"Yes." His tone is clipped. Then, with a knowing look: "This is about Rose, isn't it? Her band canceled for the lounge opening?"

I blink. "Wait—how did you know?"

"Netti told me." He leans casually against the SUV, though the glance he sneaks at his watch betrays his impatience. "Let me guess. You want me to reach out, see if he can come through last minute?"

Relief flickers in my chest. "I'd owe you."

"I'll see what I can do. No promises." He pushes off the SUV, opens the driver's door, and slides inside with that finality Connor always carries. "Goodbye, brother."

"Goodbye, Connor." I step back onto the sidewalk, tamping down the spark of excitement that he might actually fix the last snag for the lounge's grand opening. Rose and I lift our hands to wave as the SUV pulls away from the curb, disappearing into the slow flow of traffic.

We stand side by side in silence, the late-afternoon sun warm on our shoulders, until the SUV turns the corner and disappears from sight.

"You can give them a head start before heading home to save face," Rose says as she turns to head inside.

I reach out, catching her by the wrist and turning her back to me. My other hand slides up the curve of her neck, and she gasps as I cradle her cheek.

"Mhmm, I don't think so," I whisper, my lips a breath away from hers. Her pulse flutters beneath my palm. I let go of her wrist and grip her hip, pulling her flush against me. Her eyes fly open as the evidence of my arousal presses between us.

"Carter," she breathes.

I claim her lips, inhaling her sweet berry scent as I swipe my tongue against the seam of her mouth. My hand trails down her neck to her chest, grazing the swell of her breast. She moans, her body melting into mine—

And I let go, stepping back abruptly.

"You owe me dinner." I smirk, taking in her tousled hair and kiss-swollen lips from my teasing. She has no idea what she's in for tonight.

"What?" She blinks at me, staring as though I'd spoken a foreign language.

She's made me wait all these months, wanting her. It's time to turn the tables.

"You. Owe. Me. Dinner," I repeat, kicking the door closed behind me. I prowl toward her, watching the pulse flutter in her throat as her breath quickens. I don't stop until her thighs bump against the back of the couch—then pivot, brushing past her instead.

In the kitchen, I grab the jug from the fridge and pour a glass of water. The urge to drag her the few steps to her bedroom and claim my dessert first burns through me, but the cold water sliding down my throat helps clear my head.

"I heard what you said," she snaps, fire sparking in her

eyes. "Why did you"—she waves her hand between us—"stop?"

"Because." I glance at my watch, letting the pause draw out. "We have a reservation in an hour."

TRUE TO MY WORD, an hour later we're seated across from each other at the quaint yet elegant Italian restaurant. Low lighting and oak tables crowd the room, each one glowing with candlelight. Soft music drifts in the background, broken only by the occasional clink of silverware and soft murmur of conversation. A few couples linger at nearby tables, lost in their own worlds.

"I hope you're okay with my choice of restaurant," I murmur, my eyes never leaving hers as the waiter pours the best Cabernet Sauvignon on the menu into our glasses. I swirl the dark liquid, though all I'm really drinking in is her—hair curled, cascading down her back, that elegant black dress hugging every curve and leaving little to the imagination.

I'm having no trouble imagining what it would be like to peel it off her, to sink my hands into her hips and claim every inch of her.

I nearly choke on my wine.

"I ate here once—celebrating my new job, moving into my new house," Rose says as she tears off a piece of bread. She dips it into the seasoned balsamic and oil mixture and slips it between her lips. "How did you know I've always wanted to come back here?"

She could be putting something else between her lips if we'd stayed at her place.

"I have my ways." I lift my wineglass, smirking as she squirms beneath my gaze. "You look beautiful."

"Thank you." She glances down at the table, the tips of her ears reddening.

"Look at me." My voice drops to a command as I reach across the table, take her hand, and flip her palm up. Rose bites her bottom lip as she raises her eyes to meet mine. I trace my thumb along the delicate skin of her wrist, her pulse quickening under my touch. "Good girl."

Her cheeks pinken, and I release her hand, leaning back in my chair to savor the sight of her. The auburn curls spilling down her shoulders. The twitch of her lips when she's fighting her own thoughts. The heat in her eyes when she realizes I've caught her looking at me. I could spend the rest of my life memorizing her and never tire.

"What are you thinking?" she asks, taking a sip of her wine. I track the movement as her tongue flicks out to catch a drop on her bottom lip.

A growl rumbles low in my chest, my hand curling into a fist under the table to keep from leaping across it and taking her right here, right now.

"I'm thinking about what to have for dessert." My eyes trail slowly down her body, and she flushes under the weight of my scrutiny.

"Oh?" Her voice is a breathy whisper.

I love the way she responds to my attention. I can't wait to see how she reacts when I finally have time to worship every inch of her.

"What are you thinking?"

"I—" She glances around before leaning over the table, unintentionally giving me the perfect view of her lush, creamy cleavage as she whispers, "Why can't I feel your emotions or use my magic on you? I never have, not since the first day we met."

"Does it scare you?" I challenge, lifting my glass to my lips, watching her over the rim.

"That I can't feel your emotions or channel feelings to you?" She smooths the cloth napkin on her lap, considering. "No. I don't usually try to read others unless I think it would help them. I like giving people their privacy—unless they're projecting their feelings."

"That's one thing I love about you—you have such great power, but you don't abuse it."

"I'd still like to know why it doesn't work on you, though."

Probably because she doesn't know about the mating bond —and hasn't accepted it. But I can't tell her that. Not yet. Not when she's only just beginning to accept this. Accept *us*.

"Maybe it's a wolf thing?" I lean back as the waiter appears, setting our plates down. My hand tightens on my fork when his gaze lingers on Rose a second too long.

It wasn't necessary for his gaze to linger at all.

"No, because I've never had an issue with any other shifters before. Wolves included." She twirls her fettuccine and takes a bite, eyes locked on me as though daring me to explain.

"I don't know what to tell you." I dig into my spaghetti and meatballs, but the food does nothing to cool the heat burning through my veins at the thought of her touching others—even platonically. Since when did I get so damn possessive?

Since you found your mate and let her slip away.

"You're hiding something," she accuses, setting down her fork. Her gaze sharpens on me, cutting straight through. "What aren't you telling me, Carter?"

I watch her, silently observing as I continue eating. I've waited my whole life for this woman. While I'm done waiting, I can still be patient—for the right moment to broach the subject. I don't know how much she's been told, or how much she even suspects. For that matter, I don't know if non-shifters can feel the mating bond at all. I'd always meant to ask Connor, but the right time never came.

'Well?" She raises a brow, her lips pressed into a thin line. I want to lean across the table and kiss that look right off her face, but I have to admit—I'm enjoying ruffling her feathers.

"I don't know for certain," I say at last, dabbing my mouth with the cloth napkin. "I have my suspicions, but here isn't the time or place. And your food's getting cold."

She opens her mouth, then shuts it, glancing back at her plate.

"Just because you're right—and this food's too good to waste—doesn't mean I'm letting you off the hook. You'll answer my questions." She waves her fork between us before digging in again.

I could happily spend the rest of my life watching this woman across the table from me.

CHAPTER 18
ROSE

I keep sneaking glances at the man driving my car home from the restaurant. Damn shifters and their lightning metabolism. My head still hums pleasantly from the two glasses of wine at dinner. I'd wanted more—the wine burst with blackberry and cherry in every sip—but I rarely let myself indulge when I'm out, preferring to keep a level head. Carter had insisted on driving, and I was more than happy to oblige rather than risk getting behind the wheel intoxicated.

"So is it impossible to get a shifter drunk?" I ask, twisting in my seat as we pull up to a red light.

Carter keeps his eyes on the road, fingers drumming on the black leather steering wheel.

"It's not... impossible. Just extremely difficult. Especially if we're drinking only beer and wine. For a shifter, especially one in their prime, it takes some seriously strong shit." The light turns green, and we surge forward. "Why? Are you planning to get me drunk, Miss Rosemary Sinclaire? Have your wicked way with me?"

"No, of course not," I retort with mock indignation, though his teasing tone does something to my insides. I turn away, crossing my legs, ignoring the pulsing throb between my thighs.

"I know. I was just teasing." He reaches over and pats my leg, his thumb tracing slow, gentle circles on the sensitive inside of my knee. I nearly purr at the touch, but it's gone as quickly as it starts, both hands returning to the wheel.

When was the last time I felt this relaxed, this content—and wanted?

About the same time I was honest with myself about how I truly felt about this man.

I want this man. I want Carter. Not just for another weekend fling, not because I'm getting over my ex. I truly want him, and I have since the first day we met. I've been running from that truth ever since, but I'm tired of running. I know what I want.

"Carter." I turn, placing my hand on his forearm, the fine dusting of hair tickling the pads of my fingers.

"Here we are." He turns the wheel, and my hand slips to the center console as the car bumps up the curb, parking in front of my house next to his bike. "Hopefully, I wasn't too bad of a valet."

He winks before coming around to my side of the car and opening the door. I take his proffered hand, warmth enveloping mine as he helps me to my feet, my heels clacking on the cement.

"It's not your driving skills I have a problem with," I say, nodding toward his motorcycle. "It's the crotch rocket."

"She's not a crotch rocket," he chides, placing a hand over

his chest before breaking into a rumbling laugh that warms my insides. "Come on, let's get out of the cold. Spring nights still have a bite once the sun goes down."

I link my arm through his and walk steadily to my front door, digging in my purse for my keys. Ginger mewls impatiently on the other side as I slide the key into the lock and push the door open.

"Hello, baby," I coo, crouching to scratch his head. "Mommy's going to give you a special treat tonight. Oh—the to-go box!"

I stand too quickly, my heels snagging in the carpet, and stumble—but before I hit the ground, I'm caught in the familiar scent of cedarwood and bourbon, wrapped in strong arms. I look up into Carter's handsome face, my own breaking into a wide grin.

"Hello there. Nice catch."

"Hello to you too. Looking for this?" He helps me to my feet and offers the small white box holding the unseasoned slice of salmon we'd ordered to go.

"Yes, thank you." I kick off the offending heels, moaning as I wiggle my toes against the soft carpet before padding into the kitchen and setting the salmon in Ginger's bowl.

"Well, thank you for coming to dinner. I hope you enjoyed it." Carter stands in the middle of my living room, arms loose at his sides, one hand curled around the handle of his duffel. "You should get some sleep. You've only got a few days left before the grand opening."

"Wait—where are you going?"

"Well, I thought since Alexandria was gone, and you didn't need anyone to pre—"

"Wait." I cross the short distance between us and place a

hand on his chest, the other wrapped around the wrist clasping his bag. "Stay."

"Rose." His voice is gravelly and warm.

"Please." I trace a pearl-colored button on his shirt as I muster my courage. "I don't want you to go."

It's the truth. I don't want him to go—ever. I want this man, this shifter, in my life. I want to see where this thing between us could go if I gave it a chance.

"Rose." He sighs, setting his duffel on the couch and folding his arms around me. I nuzzle his chest, inhaling that intoxicating masculine scent. He presses a chaste kiss to the top of my head, then holds me at arm's length by the shoulders. "Let's get you to bed, kitten."

"But I don't want to go to bed. I want you." I pout as he takes my hand and leads me toward the bedroom.

"Teeth brushed, pajamas on, and straight to bed. If you're good, I might even tell you a story," he says, and releases my wrist, pointing to the bathroom.

"Carter." I step up, standing on my tiptoes as I wrap my arms around his neck and press my lips to his. He groans at the contact and kisses me back. His hands find my hips, pulling me against him, his obvious arousal straining at his suit pants. "Please," I whisper against his mouth.

His fingers dig into my sides as he breaks the kiss, pressing his forehead to mine, panting. "Rose, trust me—it's not that I don't want this—"

"Then let's do this." I begin unbuttoning his shirt, but he folds my hands in his, stopping me.

"Not tonight. You're not sober."

"I'm not drunk," I protest, but he cups my cheek and silences me, running a thumb over my bottom lip. The movement sends pleasant chills down my spine.

"You're not drunk, but you're not entirely sober." His hands trail like feathers around my neck until I feel the gentle tug of my zipper being pulled down and cool air touch my bare back. His fingers ghost over my skin, echoing the motion. He nips the shell of my ear, his breath a warm caress as he whispers, "If I were half the man I am, I wouldn't think twice. But I don't want to rush this, rush you. I want you, Rosemary Sinclaire, more than anything in the world."

"I want you, Carter Abernathy." I wrap my arms around myself.

"I'm not going anywhere, kitten, if you don't want me to." He kisses my forehead. "If I remember correctly, you said the bed was big enough for both of us."

He turns and walks back into the kitchen, and I move to my dresser, pulling out my comfiest silk nightdress before heading to the bathroom. I pause, a fluttering in my chest, when I see the two toothbrushes in the holder, their necks crossing where normally only mine lives. Carter must've forgotten his this morning when he packed. It feels right, seeing them there together.

Ten minutes later we're in bed, pajamas on and teeth brushed as he ordered. The silence stretches, both of us wanting and restraining.

"I'm much more sober now than when we first got home, and I haven't changed my mind," I say, leaning back against the mountain of pillows at the head of the bed, aware that the silk nightdress is sheer enough to show the blush of my nipples through the fabric.

If he's going to play hard to get, I'm going to play hard to resist.

"You're not going to change my mind," he replies, pulling my feet into his lap and pressing his thumb into the pad of my foot. I moan as pleasurable pressure radiates up my leg while his thumb works steady, firm circles along the arch.

Damn, a girl could get used to this after a night out in heels. Usually, I'm the one babying my feet the next morning, wondering whether to throw out all the torture devices or trade them in for comfortable flats.

"If you keep that up, I'll have no choice but to seduce you." It earns me a chuckle from the wolf shifter.

"Is that so?" he asks, his hand making its way up my calf. I close my eyes, delight humming through me at his touch.

It's almost sinful that a single touch can do this to me.

"Yes," I gasp, heat pooling between my legs as his hands move higher, pushing up the hem of my gown while his fingers knead the flesh of my thighs. I turn my legs outward and watch him through hooded lashes, fully aware I've just given him a front-row view of just how bare I am. His grip tightens in a delicious, painful way before releasing.

"Roll over," he commands. I open my eyes, staring at him incredulously.

"Carter," I breathe, pushing up on my elbows.

He settles one leg between mine, pressing his weight against my core. I writhe, reveling in the friction, only stoking the need building inside me. He plants a hand on either side of me, leans down, and whispers, "Not tonight, my wanton little witch. Now roll over."

He moves off and I nearly whimper at the loss of contact. He raises an eyebrow, waiting patiently until I comply and roll onto my stomach.

"Was that so hard?" he asks as he begins massaging my back, concentrating on the deep knots in my neck—knots that have tripled this week between the Wise Fox opening and hunting for Dria.

"You're a beast," I mutter into the pillow as he hits a particularly tight spot near my shoulder blade.

"I'm a wolf shifter," he growls.

My wolf shifter.

"So I've heard." I sigh, my body melting into the soft cotton sheets as he continues massaging my back, his strokes slower now, more languid. "What about my story?"

I yawn, covering my mouth before glancing over my shoulder. He smiles sleepily and lays down beside me, pulling me against his chest and tugging the blankets over us. The movement presses his rock-hard length against my back, and my core starts throbbing all over again. I shift my hips, searching for even a shred of relief. There's no way I'm falling asleep like this.

"Rose." Carter's voice, deep as sin, is a hot caress on my neck.

"I need—" I rub my thighs together, but it does nothing to ease the ache building inside me. I feel too tight in my own skin, every brush of the sheets or the wolf behind me stoking the fire higher.

Well, if he's not going to break, I'll just have to do it myself.

I run my hand down my chest, pinching a nipple.

"Stubborn little witch," Carter whispers against my neck as his hand slips between my thighs. I arch at the contact, magic thrumming through my veins as he slides two fingers deep inside. His thumb draws slow, deliberate circles over my clit, sending rippling waves coursing through me.

"Stubborn big bad wolf," I moan, arching into his touch, wanting more—needing more. The orgasm builds fast, ready to crest. "Please, I need more. I need you."

He nips at my shoulder and pauses his ministrations. I squirm, denied the release I was so close to.

"You'll have me," he growls into the sensitive crook of my neck, "but tonight you'll ride my fingers. And if tomorrow you still feel the same, I'll let you ride my face." He pushes up to sit.

I gasp, my cheeks heating at his words and the images he plants in my head. Then his fingers begin pumping in and out of me again, faster now, his rhythm steady and relentless.

"More," I beg breathlessly. Carter leans over, mouth hot as he runs his tongue over my left nipple. I gasp, thrusting my chest forward as he nips the peak, drawing it deep into his mouth, working magic with his tongue while his fingers play me like an instrument.

I shatter into a million pieces, stars bursting behind my eyelids as wave after wave of pleasure courses through me.

Carter slowly withdraws and settles behind me, pulling me possessively to his chest, palm pressed flat over my heart.

"Good night, kitten." He kisses the bare skin of my shoulder. I part my lips to speak, but the words slip away as sleep claims me.

CHAPTER 19
CARTER

I wake to a deep, rumbling purr and the heavy warmth of a small body on my chest. Peeking one eye open, I spot a tumble of auburn hair tucked beneath my arm and perched right over my heart, a tiny orange furball staring at me with wide, bright blue eyes.

"Good morning, Ginger," I murmur. The cat licks his paw, shooting me a sidelong glance as if to say, *It's about time, human. I'm starving.* The warmth is pleasant enough, but the tiny claws kneading my skin are less so. I don't want to move, not with Rose's breath soft against my side.

"Fine," I grumble, swinging my legs over the edge of the bed as the cool air shocks my skin. I try to disentangle myself without waking her, Ginger's purr vibrating against my arm.

"Where are you going?" she mumbles, her eyes blinking open.

I hold up Ginger, who peers at me, purr intensifying like

I've been caught stealing. "Your furry orange menace is hangry."

"I'm so sorry," Rose says, her gaze dropping to the tiny scratches on my chest, lips pursing. "He can be grumpy sometimes, but he means well. He's just a baby."

"I'll be right back. Do you want anything?" I pause in the doorway, scratching Ginger's head, the soft fur a comforting texture beneath my fingers.

"You," she answers, her voice laced with a hunger that has my morning wood stirring harder than it already was. Her eyes flick down to my favorite appendage straining against my briefs.

I chuckle before heading to the kitchen. After filling Ginger's bowl, the clinking of kibble the only sound in the otherwise quiet house, I make a beeline back to the bedroom. Rose sits up in bed, auburn hair a fiery halo around her face as the morning light catches the strands. Two quick strides and I'm at her side, our lips colliding in a fervent kiss that leaves us both breathless.

"Goddess, you're beautiful," I whisper, tucking a strand of hair behind her ear. She closes her eyes, leaning into my touch as I trace my hand down the line of her temple to her jaw. "Did you mean it?"

Her eyes open, locking with mine.

"Of course I did. I told you last night—"

"Oh, thank goodness. I worried all night you'd change your mind about quitting our jobs and running away to join the circus. Let's get packed."

I pull back, watching her brows pinch together.

"What?"

"Run away with me and join the circus," I repeat, failing to hide my grin when she slaps my chest.

"I did *not* agree to that. I said nothing of the sort."

"Well, you know—you had quite a few glasses of wine and were pretty drunk."

"I was *not* drunk last night, and you know it. What are you playing at, Carter?"

I grab her legs and pull her to the edge of the bed. She squeaks, flailing as she falls back, propped on her elbows.

"Oh, I know." I wedge myself between her knees, and her breath hitches. Her eyes never leave mine as my hands trail lightly up her thighs. I lean down and ghost a kiss over her lips. "Tell me you don't want this. Tell me to pack my bags and I'll leave."

Even if it might kill me to let you walk away again.

"Carter, I *want* this. I want you. Please."

"Good," I growl, nipping her neck before trailing kisses down until I take one of her nipples into my mouth, flicking the bud with my tongue. Rose arches, and I move to the other breast, lavishing it with attention. I work my way lower, worshipping her body with kisses until I'm on my knees before her. She giggles as I lift her legs over my shoulders, taking in my fill of the gorgeous spread before me. Sliding my hands beneath her, I squeeze her ass as I bury my face in her core. She moans, thighs wrapping around my head.

"I love the way you taste."

"More," she demands, arching on the bed, her fingers grazing my scalp and pressing me closer.

"Bossy today, aren't we, kitten?" I nip at her inner thigh, glancing up at her lust-glossed eyes.

"You're the one who made me wait all night," she pants as I slip a finger through her folds, taunting her.

You're the one who made me wait over a year.

I take my time, leisurely stroking her, worshiping her with

my tongue. She cries out, fists clenching the sheets, hips bucking wildly as she winds into release.

"Damnit, Carter, get in me already."

"Bossy *and* impatient. Maybe I should've fed you first," I growl, pushing down my briefs as I rise to my feet. Her eyes rove hungrily down my chest, landing on my shaft as I wrap a hand around it, stroking myself.

"I do like breakfast." Her tongue darts out to lick her bottom lip as she moves to sit up, but I press a hand to her shoulder, my thumb caressing the pulse in her throat as I ease her back down onto the bed.

"Not today." My hand drifts down her silk nightgown, sliding between her thighs as I push two fingers inside, setting a steady pace. "One day I'll see that sassy mouth of yours wrapped around my cock, but this morning is all about you."

I pull my fingers free and reach for my jeans, pulling out a condom and rolling it down my length before lining myself up at her entrance.

"Now who's the bossy one?"

Leaning down, I brace an arm beside her head and lick up the curve of her neck, savoring the salty taste of her skin.

"I can never get enough of the taste of you," I growl against the shell of her ear.

"Oh? What do I taste like?" she breathes, writhing impatiently beneath me.

Her gasps tears through the room as I fist a handful of her hair and sink into her with one sharp thrust.

Mine.

"Like warm summer berries under a full moon." I hold still above her as she adjusts to my girth, admiring the way her hair fans out like a dark, fiery halo around her head. "A sweet, saccharine treat—every bite leaves me craving more."

Her cheeks flush, lashes fluttering against freckled skin.

"Cat got your tongue?"

"Carter," she moans, pressing back against me, biting her bottom lip.

"Look at me, Rose." Her eyes snap open at my command, and I begin to pump slow and deep, holding her gaze captive. "I'm going to take my time, kitten."

"Gods, Carter," she cries, her nails raking down my back.

"You keep doing that, and I won't be able to play nice." The primal urge to bite and claim her surges through me, but I force myself to stay focused on her.

"Your eyes are nearly golden." She cups my cheek, her thumb brushing the rough stubble at my jaw.

"You bring the wolf out in me," I rumble before claiming her mouth in a kiss that's all teeth, tongue, and raw passion, pouring everything I've held back into her. When we break apart, both of us are panting, eyes locked.

"They say, 'Beware the big bad wolf,'" she whispers, threading her fingers through my hair and tightening her grip. "But I think I might just be falling for you, Carter Abernathy."

I admire the way her swollen lips curl into a grin. "Just think? I'll have to do better, then."

She squeals as I roll to my back, bringing her with me until she settles on top of me, buried deep inside her and enveloped by her warmth. Eyes closed in ecstasy, Rose throws her head back, hands clutching my chest, a low moan spilling from her lips. I thrust my hips in a gentle rhythm, restraining the frantic need to take her until she can't walk for a week. "You like that?"

"Like it? I lo—" Her eyes widen as I cup her breasts, my thumbs rubbing over her peaked nipples. Her hips become jerky as she rides me, and I drop a hand between her thighs, circling her clit. She cries out, clawing at my shoulders as her core milks me, sending me over the edge.

She rolls over to face me and nestles closer, one leg draped over mine. Her fingers weave through the fine dusting of hair on my chest as I trace featherlight circles along her shoulder. "That was amazing," she whispers, her smile warm against my skin.

"I know I am," I say with a smirk—which earns me a smack to the chest. "Hey! That's no way to treat your—"

I bite back the word *mate* before it slips out and close my eyes, groaning inwardly. So much has been going on; there hasn't been the right time to talk about that.

"My what?" Rose asks, pushing up and staring down at me. Her face is glowing, hair tousled, lips swollen.

"Your—" I fumble for a witty reply, but my mind goes blank. My wolf—content to be in his mate's bed—has gone quiet.

"What are we exactly, Carter?" She nibbles her bottom lip as she studies me.

"What do you want us to be, Rose?"

You ran away from me. I've always been here, waiting.

Her eyes drop to my chest and my gut clenches, waiting for the rejection—waiting for her to run again. The silence stretches on, heavy and slow, even though only minutes pass.

"Do you..." She looks up and meets my gaze, her nose wrinkling in that cute little face she makes when she's struggling for words. Rarely have I seen Rose flustered, and I'm fascinated watching her process the question. "I mean, would you like to be—"

Just say yes and kiss the girl.

"Your personal bodyguard?" I grin wolfishly at her.

More like a friendly neighborhood guard dog who wants to rip a certain ex limb from limb.

"Carter, I'm being serious," she says exasperatedly, though the corner of her lips still quirks as she rolls her eyes and chuckles.

"Rose, I'm yours for as long as you'll have me. If you want to date, we date. If down the road you want more, then we'll have that conversation."

She gasps as I flip her onto her back, pinning her wrists above her head as I crouch over her. I nuzzle the side of her face, scent marking her. Not that I hadn't already done it a dozen times this morning as I worshipped every inch her body.

"What I don't want is to lose you again."

CHAPTER 20
ROSE

"Carter?" I call, pulling my robe tighter around my shoulders, my bare feet padding softly across the cold tile as I tiptoe into the kitchen.

Ginger meows and rolls onto his side where he's been sunning himself in the light streaming through the window. Bending down, I scratch under his fluffy orange-and-white chin, rewarded with a deep, rumbling purr.

Straightening, I reach for a mug when I spot a note on the counter in Carter's familiar scrawl.

Rose,
Ran out to run a few errands and give you some time to work. I'll be back around one for lunch. — Carter

As I reread the note, warmth blooms in my chest; I inhale

deeply, the paper carrying the faintest whisper of his cedar-wood-and-vanilla scent. Waking in his arms and spending the whole day getting to know each other again would've been ideal, but he has a point. The lounge opening is tomorrow, and I have a mountain of preparations to tackle after the chaos of the past few days threw everything off schedule.

Still, all I want is a break—one spent in his arms.

"First things first, let's check in with the bakery before I try to fix this decorations mess." After typing in the store's number, I press call and lift the receiver to my ear. It rings and rings before flipping to voicemail.

"Maisel's Macarons. We are with other customers at the moment. Please provide your name and number so we can call you back as soon as possible."

The phone emits a loud beep.

"Good morning. This is Rosemary Sinclaire. I have an order placed for tomorrow for the Wise Fox Lounge opening. I just wanted to call and confirm everything is still on track to be delivered."

I set the phone face down on the counter, unease twisting low in my stomach.

"It's just pre-event jitters, Rose. Pull yourself together. They're probably just busy and will call back. Focus on the real problem at hand—those blasted chartreuse decorations."

As the coffee pot begins to brew, I dial the number of a childhood friend. Angela picks up on the third ring.

"Rosemary! I haven't heard from you in ages," she says warmly. "Is everything alright?"

"Hey, Ange. Sorry I've been distant—I've been up to my neck in projects and work."

"You always were a busy bee—even in school, making sure everyone and every detail was just right." She chuckles, and I wince at the sound of children in the background. I've been so wrapped up in my projects and work, everyone I used to know has gone on to start families of their own. A tug pulls at my chest as my thoughts stray to Carter, wondering if children are something he's ever wanted. From what Netti's told me, he's never settled down.

"That's actually why I'm calling. I'm juggling multiple events, and there's been a mistake with the decorations."

"You're going to work yourself to death one of these days, Rose. How can I help?"

"Well, the decorations are chartreuse green, and they're supposed to be cerulean blue. Somehow, the store has been completely bought out of blue stock and can't substitute," I explain, drumming my fingers on the counter.

"So you've got a mountain of ugly green decorations and need them to be blue?"

"Yes, exactly. And I vividly remember you charming the homecoming decorations into opal—shifting between every color of the rainbow for our under-the-sea theme. You always had top scores in transfiguration."

"You flatter me, Rose—but that is true. I suppose I could come out and see what I can do. When's your event? A week? A month?"

"Tomorrow."

"Tomorrow?"

My stomach twists in knots as the phone falls silent.

"Angela?"

"Rose, I really want to help you. I do, but with two small boys under three, I can't drop everything to fly out."

"I know. I knew it was a long shot, but I figured I'd try. Thank you."

"Have you tried Marcelene? Let me text you her number."

"Not yet, but I'll give her a call."

An hour and two cups of coffee later, I've called half the witch contacts I've met over the years. Either their skills in illumination weren't up to the task, or they had other obligations and couldn't fly out on such short notice.

I sigh, pick up one of the putrid green balloons, and scrunch my nose as I concentrate, pulling on the magic in and around me. Although I don't know any spells to change an object's color, some magic can be coaxed with focused intention.

"Make it blue, make it blue," I whisper under my breath. My fingers tingle as I think of the sky, the ocean, even Carter's blasted blue bike. I peek one eye open, and a wave of disappointment washes over me when the atrocious green balloon in my hand remains unchanged.

"Maybe she won't even notice in the lounge's dim interior?" I mutter to Ginger, who gives me a single glance before returning to a thorough lick of his paw.

"I'll take that as a no."

"Take what as a no?"

I jump and spin, my heart racing—and then a grin spreads across my face at the sound of Carter's voice.

"You're back! Oh, here, let me help you with that." I rush to his side, grab the drink tray from his hands, and carry it to the kitchen. He leans over and plants a kiss on my cheek, the scruff of his beard brushing my skin.

"Sorry, I need to shave, but I didn't want to wake you this morning," he says, cupping my face, his thumb rasping gently along my jaw.

"Don't be sorry. It looks good on you."

I only hope he doesn't see the lovesick look plastered across my face. Every moment with him, I feel more at ease.

More comfortable in my own skin. Like sunshine on a warm day.

"How are preparations for the lounge going?" Carter moves through the kitchen with ease, grabbing two plates and setting down flaky, buttery croissant sandwiches after tossing his bags on the couch. "Don't worry, I didn't forget about you."

He pops open a can of cat food and places it on a tray on the floor. Ginger prances over, tail flicking as he all but inhales the meal.

"You're going to spoil him," I chide, picking up one of the sandwiches.

"This cute face?" He lifts the scrambling kitten before setting him back beside his food offering. "You're deflecting."

"I'm not deflecting, I'm eating." I nod toward his untouched sandwich, licking crumbs from my fingers.

"Maybe I'm hungry for something else," he purrs, voice husky as he catches my wrist. My insides nearly melt when he licks my fingers clean, then drops my hand only to tug me against him. A breath escapes me, lips parting—and then his mouth is on mine.

Our tongues tangle, teasing, his hands roaming my back. I'm consumed, yet utterly full, as Carter kisses me like his life depends on it. A thrill races through me, my magic humming over my skin, though I still can't read his emotions.

The buzz of my phone shatters the moment. We break apart, panting. Heat floods my face as I fumble through my purse for the blasted device, torn between gratitude for the reprieve and disappointment at the interruption.

"Rosemary?"

"This is she," I reply, hoping I don't sound as breathless as I feel.

"This is Maisel from Maisel's Macarons." I blow out a

breath and run my fingers through my hair, turning away from Carter.

"Oh, Mrs. Maisel. Thank you so much for returning my call. I just wanted to confirm everything was on track for tomorrow's event." I begin pacing the length of my small kitchen.

"Well, honey, that's why I'm calling." In the distance I hear sirens. "Unfortunately, there was a little accident—our main oven caught on fire. Everyone is safe, but the kitchen will be down for at least a week. I can issue you a refund for your deposit, or you can apply it toward a future order."

My stomach plummets. First my car, then the wrong color decorations, the band canceling—and now no macarons. I was a dead witch. No, worse than a dead witch. This could end my career if word got out.

"Rosemary, are you still there?" Maisel asks.

"Sorry, a refund of the deposit will be fine. Thank you for letting me know." I hit *end* on the call and slowly sink to the floor, covering my face with my hands.

This is it. I'm ruined. This was my last chance to salvage the opening night, and now it's doomed to fail. No amount of magic or money can fix this.

"Rose?" Carter's warm hands squeeze my shoulders as he kneels beside me. I peer into his bright blue eyes, my head resting against the wooden cabinets.

"I'm ruined. The event is ruined." I bury my face in my hands, but he pries them away, tilts my chin up, and forces me to meet his gaze.

"What happened?" His voice is a soothing balm to my senses, and I blink away unshed tears.

"There was an accident at the bakery." My voice cracks on the last syllable. "They canceled the macaron order."

"Well, why don't you call another bakery?"

"It doesn't work like that. You can't just call another bakery and have ten dozen custom macarons ready the next day."

"Well, why don't we make them?"

"You don't just—" I laugh at the absurdity and wave at my tiny kitchen from his lap. "First, this is not an industrial bakery. And second, I might be a witch, but I can't wave my magic wand around and make miracles happen."

"You have a magic wand?"

"You know what I mean." I start to stand, but he pulls me right back into his lap.

"I know." He cradles my face in his hands, pressing gentle kisses to my forehead, eyelids, and then cheeks. "Let's just make them."

"Have you ever made macarons before?"

"No, but they can't be that hard." He helps me to my feet with a shrug.

"I don't know the first thing about making macarons."

"Well, it's a good thing you know someone who does." He reaches behind me, grabs my phone, and presses it into my hand.

***

"Are you sure you don't want me to drive up?" My phone is cradled between my ear and shoulder as I jot down the last of Netti's tips. My small couch is already overflowing with bags—we'd hit two grocery stores and a bakery supply shop to get everything on her list.

"No, I've got it. By the time you get here, it'll be past midnight. You rest up, and I'll see you tomorrow."

"Is that Rose and Carter?" Connor's voice comes faintly through the speaker, muffled by background noise.

"Yes," Netti answers, clearly half-covering the mic. "There

was a little... incident with the macarons. I'm just walking them through how to fix it."

"My brother, baking macarons?" Connor snorts, the sound sharp enough to make me press a hand to my mouth, stifling a laugh. "I'd pay good money to see that."

Before I can retort, his voice comes through clearer as if Netti handed him the phone. "Anyway, I've actually got good news. Rose?"

"I'm here," I say quickly.

"Netti mentioned your band canceled. If you're still looking, an old friend of mine's in town. His band said they'd love to fill the spot. I'll text you their info and a link to their page."

Relief washes over me. "That would be perfect! I've been calling around all day, and everyone else is booked out for weeks—sometimes months."

"Then it's settled."

"Alright, give me that back—Rose doesn't have all night to yap," Netti cuts in, and there's a playful scuffle on the other end.

I smile into the phone. "You'll have to give Connor an extra big hug for me. I'd already given up hope on finding another band. Now I just have to figure out how to whip up dozens of macarons before tomorrow."

"You've got this. Just don't overmix the batter, as tempting as it is," Netti warns.

"I know, I know. You've already told me." I tap my fingers anxiously on the counter.

"And call me if you run into any trouble."

I glance over at the man in my kitchen, popping blueberries into his mouth while dangling one of Ginger's toys above him. Trouble had walked through my door, but I wasn't in any hurry for it to leave.

"I promise I will. Sleep well, and drive safe in the morning," I say before hanging up and turning to Carter. "Are you ready for this?"

"I'm at your command," he replies with a mock bow, picking up a bowl and whisk. "As long as I get to lick the whisk at the end—and any frosting you splatter on yourself. Or that I splatter on you."

Laughing, I shake my head and snatch the bowl and whisk from him.

"While I don't doubt your strength, we're going to need more than a handheld whisk."

I bend down and search the cupboard, finally unearthing my grandmother's old stand mixer and setting it on the counter. A fine layer of dust clings to the surface, but otherwise it looks in good order.

"That thing's got to be a hundred years old. Does it even work?" Carter swipes a finger through the dust before inspecting the cord.

"Let's hope so. Otherwise, we're either skipping arm day for a week or heading to the department store for a new one." I chuckle, tossing the bowl and whisk head into the sink of soapy water before scrubbing down the machine.

"Where'd you even get it?" He takes the bowl from me, rinses, and dries it with a dish towel.

"It was my grandma's. She insisted I'd need it when I left for college. I've never taken it out except to move it—until now. I guess she was right."

Once we piece it back together, I whisper a silent prayer, plug it in, and flip the switch. The machine hums to life, the whisk spinning with a comforting whir, and I let out a breath of relief. At least something is finally going my way—a small victory in a sea of setbacks.

"So it says first we have to separate the egg whites to make the meringue. Netti said if we use the Italian method it'll create a more billowy meringue and make it less likely for the batter to deflate while baking." I dig through the bags until I find the egg separator and hand it to him along with three bowls. "She also said to separate one egg at a time in case the yolk breaks, so none slips into the whites."

Carter sets to the task while I read through the recipe for the dozenth time. I carefully measure the granulated sugar and water, bringing it to 245 degrees. When the egg whites reach soft peaks, I slowly drizzle in the bubbling syrup, adding a pinch of cream of tartar as the stand mixer whirs.

"I think this looks right." I stop the mixer and peer at the silken mixture.

"See, you can do anything." Carter beams as he comes up behind me, resting his hands on my hips and pressing a kiss to the top of my head.

"Ha! This is just the halfway point. Pass me the almond flour, powder sugar, and blue coloring." He steps away, and I feel the sudden absence of his warmth.

I fold in the sifted dry ingredients and coloring, gently mixing until the batter ribbons off my spatula in a slow, wide stream.

"Here goes nothing." I load the mixture into piping bags and begin filling the little circles on the baking liner, the bright blue batter a bold contrast against the silver sheet. At least they'll be uniform.

"Those look delicious.," Carter murmurs, reaching out to touch one of the mounds—but I swat his hand away.

"They aren't ready yet!" I grab the tray and lift it a few inches before dropping it back onto the counter. The metal clatters sharply against the stone surface.

"What did you do that for? I thought they needed to be fluffy," he says, brow furrowing.

"Netti said we need to do that to let the bubbles out before they form a skin."

Making macarons has been the strangest experiment—not that I've done much baking in my life. Outside of standard staples, I was always more than content to support small shops. Now, I've gained a whole new appreciation for them.

"She knows better than me," he says with a shrug, turning to wash the bowls in the sink.

"Let's just hope she's right." My gut twists as I stare at the trays lined with two dozen blue circles of cookie batter. At least they weren't green. "One dozen down, nine more to go."

"As long as I'm with you, I don't care what we're doing." Carter cups my cheek and brushes a gentle kiss across my lips.

I nearly melt right there with the way he looks at me, like I'm the moon to his sky.

"It'll be midnight before we finish these." I drop my gaze, toeing the floor.

"Then we'll eat midnight macarons. I won't fail you, Rosemary." His arms wrap around me, warm and sure, and I feel the truth in his words.

CHAPTER 21
CARTER

"I couldn't have done this without you," Rose says as she turns toward me after loading the last box of macarons into the trunk of her car.

"I'm sure you would've figured it out. You're a smart witch." I tap the tip of her nose before scooping her into my arms. She squeals as I spin her around before setting her gently back on her feet.

"We fixed the macaron disaster, but what about the decorations?" Her lips dip at the corners, brow furrowing. "She's going to kill me if I show up with either no decorations or these..."

She flips open the cardboard box and plucks out a putrid green balloon between her finger and thumb. Her nose wrinkles, shoulders sagging, deflated as the rubber in her hand.

"Hey." I catch her by the hips, pulling her tight against my chest as I wrap her up and press a kiss to the top of her head. "I have a few ideas. Let's just get these cookies to the lounge and into the fridge."

"They aren't just cookies, they're macarons. But you have a point." She glances at the rising sun, then back at the trunk. "We need to get them chilled before it gets any warmer."

"I can think of a few things to make it warmer," I whisper, sliding my hands down to cup her ass.

"Carter!" She slaps my chest and shakes her head, pulling free of my grasp. I reluctantly let her go.

"Go on, get going."

"You're not coming?" Her brows pinch as I reach up and shut the trunk.

"I'm coming. I just need to make a few phone calls and run an errand. I'll catch up." I brush a kiss across her lips, then gently turn her by the shoulders toward the driver's door. I wave as she pulls out of the driveway, watching until the car disappears before pulling out my phone.

Scrolling through my contacts, I find the witch I'm looking for and dial. Fernando answers on the third ring.

"Carter, what a surprise," he says in his soft German accent.

"I'm calling in that favor. How fast can you get to the Wise Fox Lounge in Greyhaven?" I'd checked in with him a few days ago to see where in the world he was residing, and bless the goddess, he was only an hour away.

"For you? Two hours." I hear the rustle of fabric and nearly roll my eyes. Of course, the witch is still in bed. He probably stayed up all night.

Ending the call and tucking my phone into my pocket, I double-check Rose's front door. Her protection wards are in place, but I wouldn't put it past her ex to pull some bullshit while we're gone. I circle the perimeter of the yard, shifter senses sharpened, searching for the faintest trace of anything amiss in the air or ground.

Ours to protect. Ours to guard.

"I know." My teeth grind together as a strange sense of premonition washes over me.

AN HOUR AND A HALF LATER, I dismount my bike and, with a reassuring pat, check my breast pocket to make sure the small package survived the ride. Nestled inside is a blue topaz set in the crook of a white-gold crescent moon, strung on a delicate chain. The moment I'd seen it in the jewelry store window, while I was supposed to be looking for the wolf pup, I knew it belonged around my Rosemary's neck. More than just a necklace, though, it's been warded with protection spells.

"Rose?" I push open the heavy wooden doors to the lounge and am assaulted by the sight of chartreuse runners draped across tables, each topped with vases of blue and cream flowers. If not for the garish green clashing against the décor, the space—with its blue walls and mahogany wood paneling—would be warm, inviting. The kind of place I could see myself frequenting often. But my attention locks on the center of the room, where my witch stands on a ladder, fastening a garland to the ceiling beams. She glances over her shoulder, her expression faltering.

"It's that bad, isn't it?" she asks as she climbs down, raking her fingers through her hair.

"I told her once the lights are dimmed, the band starts playing, and folks have a few drinks in them, they won't care what color the decorations are," the burly man behind the bar says as he polishes a glass and sets it on the neatly arranged shelf behind him. The shelves are lined with rows of bottles in various shades of blue, glowing faintly under the recessed ceiling lamps.

"The people might not care, but *she* will. You've known her for years, Charlee. She'll never trust me to run another event again." Rose lets out a hiccupped laugh before burying her face in her hands.

"Kitten, I'm sure it's not going to be that bad. The green gives it a—" I glance around the room, searching for the right words. "Fresh, hip vibe?"

"You mean like what my great-aunt Frieda's cat puked up after getting into the dumpsters?" Fernando's rich voice calls from the front door, and my shoulders sag in relief.

"Not exactly the words I was going for—"

"That's because you're trying to sugarcoat it, wolf, for this beautiful dame." He bows deeply to Rose before straightening and grasping my hand, shaking it fervently.

"I'm sorry, but the lounge doesn't open for a few more hours."

"Didn't Carter tell you?" Fernando quirks an eyebrow.

"What didn't you tell me?" Rose turns to me, confusion clouding her features.

"Well, I did mention I had some phone calls to make and errands to run." I resist the urge to reach into my pocket. Now isn't the right time.

"What wolf boy is trying to say is that I'm here to save the day." Fernando smirks, pearly white teeth flashing in the light.

"The only thing that could save today would be a truck full of blue decorations—or a team of witches to enchant everything before tonight's opening."

"Well then, you're in luck." He lays a hand on the nearest table, and with a wiggle of his pinky, cerulean ink spreads across the runner in intricate swirling patterns until not a speck of green remains.

Rose's eyes widen. She hurries to the table, running her hand along the fabric before looking up at him.

"That's... fascinating." She glances over her shoulder. "But this is just one runner. We have an entire lounge to fix. The amount of magic—"

"I've got enough. But first, I need a drink. I nearly felt like I was flying—I drove so fast to make it here on time."

"If you're here to help our Rose, the first drink's on the house. What'll it be, mate?" Charlee calls from behind the bar.

"Gin and tonic with a splash of lime, please." Fernando laces his fingers together, stretching his arms overhead before letting out a low whistle. "You weren't kidding, wolf. This is quite the dig. I'll have to reach out to the owner."

"What is it exactly that you do? And how do you know Carter?"

"Well, what I do is a conversation for another time. As for how I know this handsome man? He saved my ass years ago. I never thought he'd call in the favor I promised him."

"ARE you sure you can't stay for the opening?" Rose asks as we stand by the front door with Fernando.

"Unfortunately, I have business I must return to. But I have a feeling I'll be seeing you around." He dabs the sheen of sweat from his forehead, then waves and heads for the sleek black sedan parked beside my bike.

We stand side by side, watching until he disappears down the road. Rose glances at her watch.

"Two hours until opening. The band is finishing their

sound check. We've got a few minutes to freshen up before I double-check—"

I pull her face to mine, silencing her with a kiss. Brushing a stray lock from her cheek, I reach down to entwine our fingers.

"Everything is perfect. Let's go freshen up. I put together some food while you and Fernando were finishing."

Hand in hand, we walk into the back hall, and I hold open the drapery that serves as the room's door. Rose gasps, her hand flying to her mouth as the warm glow of dozens of candles washes over her. The small table in the center is laden with carefully piled cheese, fragrant meats, crunchy nuts, and plump, sweet grapes.

"Carter, this is—"

"You've been working so hard. I wanted to take care of you." I brush her hair off her shoulder, and she melts back against me, baring her neck. If only she knew what that subtle, submissive gesture did to me. I nip lightly at the delicate skin, resisting the urge to bite her. To mark her.

She's ours. Tell her. Claim her.

"Carter," she gasps, arching as I run my hands along her front, caressing the swell of her breasts before settling on her hips, pulling her back until her ass grinds against the arousal straining my slacks.

"I have something for you, but you have to promise to be good." I release her and pull the little box from my pocket, dangling the necklace before her. "Tonight, I want to see you in nothing but the moon on your skin."

She caresses the cool metal as I fasten the necklace around her throat. A wicked smile tugs at the corners of her mouth as she turns in my arms.

"We have two hours—"

"To eat and get ready." I sit on the plush couch and pull her into my lap, then reach forward to grab a square of Brie. "Open."

Rose obliges, parting her lips, and I feed her the small chunk. "Good girl." I reward her with a quick kiss. We finish the rest of the spread in companionable silence, taking turns feeding each other—intimate in its own way, shared with my mate.

"Thank you," she whispers as I help her to her feet and grab the garment bags from the coat rack.

"You don't need to thank me. I want to be your solid rock, your partner. I want you to thrive and blossom, and I want to do it all by your side."

"I think I'd like that," she says.

I nuzzle her cheek and the hollow of her neck, inhaling her intoxicating berry-and-cream scent. I'll never get enough of this witch.

"What are you doing? That tickles!" she squeals, squirming in my arms.

"Scent marking you, so every supernatural being here tonight knows you're mine," I growl in her ear, taking her hand. "Now, kitten—let's get dressed. We have a party to attend."

CHAPTER 22
CARTER

"Angelique, I'd love for you to meet Carter." Rose beams as she gestures between us, her eyes sparkling as if she's both proud and nervous. The tall, lithe blonde moves toward us with the kind of effortless grace that comes from knowing the entire room bends to her will. And why wouldn't it? She owns the place.

"It's a pleasure," I say, inclining my head politely. "I've heard great things from Rose."

Angelique's lips curve. "It is I who should be praising her." She sweeps a hand around the lounge. "The house is packed, there's a line down the block, and this place looks better than any concept we discussed."

"Rose, true to her name, makes beauty bloom," I add, my voice low but steady. I brush my knuckles lightly against the back of her hand, feeling the heat that floods her skin. "Have you tried her macarons?"

"They were divine," Angelique replies, eyes alight. "I'll need them catered again. But what do you mean by hers?" She glances at Rose.

Rose's gaze drops, her cheeks pinkening. "There was, um... an incident with the bakery. So Carter and I made them ourselves."

"Rosemary Sinclaire," Angelique chides gently, catching her hands with a laugh, "what other hidden talents are you keeping from me? Aside from this handsome wolf shifter Charlee says is always at your side?"

Rose's blush deepens, and she stammers, "It wasn't meant to be a secret—I had things handled, but—"

"She did more than handle it," I cut in smoothly, unwilling to let her minimize herself. My arm brushes hers, steady, grounding. "Rose pulled off in a week what most people couldn't do in a month. Tonight is her vision—her dedication—that's why it's a success."

Angelique's eyes soften as she pats Rose's hands. "Take ease, little witch. Your wolf is right. This night would not be the triumph it is without you. Most would have buckled under that pressure, but you"—she gestures toward the crowd—"you kept your head and played your team to their strengths. That's leadership."

Rose dares a quick glance up at me, her grin wide, eyes shining with a pride she tries to hide. "Thank you. Truly. This opening might be the talk of the town. People will come from everywhere to see your lounge."

"You, my dear, will be the talk of the town." Angelique gestures discreetly toward a group across the room. "I've had at least five people already ask for your contact."

"Five? Me?" Rose's voice pitches higher in disbelief.

I can't help the smile tugging at my lips. "Told you," I murmur, low enough that only she hears.

Angelique raises a brow. "What do you think, little witch? I have projects all over the globe. Should I keep you to myself?"

Rose's fingers twist nervously in front of her. "I'd be delighted to do more projects with you."

"Good." Angelique squeezes her arm, then glances at me. "Do you mind if I steal Rose away? There are people desperate to meet her."

"Be my guest," I reply, though my chest tightens as Angelique whisks her away, my mate glowing under the praise. I watch her—head high now, confidence finally breaking through her meekness—and can't help thinking she's never looked more beautiful.

Only when they disappear into the crowd do I turn back to the bar. Charlee's waiting with a whiskey on ice, sliding it toward me with a knowing grin.

I toss back the drink, the burn clawing down my throat until it pools warm in my belly. The glass is empty save for the single half-melted ice sphere that clinks softly as I twirl it. I slide the glass down the bar; Charlee snatches it without looking, already turning back to the crowd with the sleek confidence of a predator who owns the room. Muscles ripple beneath his rolled cuffs as he pours two pints and slides them to a pair of shifters.

"What can I get you all tonight?" he asks, a grin tugging one corner of his mouth.

"The house special!" the gathered crowd shouts over the music from the stage.

He arches a brow as he sets a silver-and-crystal cocktail shaker on the bar to a round of hoots and whistles. With practiced ease, he splashes a medley of spirits from the bottles behind him, adds a dash of edible glitter powder, then snaps on the lid and sends the shaker arcing into the air. It spins, scattering glints of turquoise, gold, and amber beneath the lounge's low lights, and for a heartbeat every eye in the room tilts upward to watch it drop neatly into his waiting grip. "Enjoy."

He lines half a dozen coupe glasses on the counter and fills them to the brim before the crowd erupts in cheers and applause.

I turn away from the spectacle, leaning back against the bar, my fingers brushing the counter. My eyes immediately find my mate across the room, her head tossed back in laughter as she points toward the band and then around at various features of the lounge. She's practically glowing—and it's more than the subtle lighting. She catches my gaze as though she feels the burn of my eyes on her skin. Her cheeks flush, and she bites her bottom lip before breaking the contact and returning to her companions.

I could think of better ways to spend time with our mate right now.

While I don't disagree, there's plenty of time to explore the scenario already running through my mind.

"She really is something, isn't she?" Charlee says from behind me, and it's all I can do not to flinch. Had I let my guard down so much I hadn't even heard him approach?

"Yeah, she is." I glance over my shoulder.

"She's going to have her hands full after this. Everyone will be knocking at her door. She'll have opportunities to travel the world."

"She deserves it." The words scrape out of me, softer than I intend.

His bushy, peppered brow arches as he pours, amber liquid

catching the dim light. "And you? What's your place in all this?"

"I'll go anywhere she goes," I answer as I take the proffered glass. But as soon as my fingers curl around the cold surface, a sour twist of anxiety knots in my chest.

Something isn't right.

Rose.

I spin around in my chair, eyes darting across the floor, but she's gone—vanished. My heart hammers like a drum, each beat igniting the wolf beneath my skin. He prowls, tense and restless, drawn by a fierce, urgent need to find her, protect her.

My little mate.

"Carter?" Charlee's voice slices through the animalistic haze clouding my mind, and I whip around, senses on fire.

"Did you see where she went?" I growl, hands tipped with claws, knuckles whitening on the bar.

"No. I'm sorry, mate. Perhaps she stepped into the back. I'll keep an eye out."

"Thank you." I toss back the whiskey, fire burning down my throat, then snap to my feet. That's when it hits me—the acrid, familiar sting of his stale cologne. Her ex.

My mate.

Rage claws at my chest.

Rip him limb from limb.

"We can't just go around disembodying people," I mutter, forcing control as I barrel down the back hall, following the trail of scent. Every nerve hums, shifter senses sharp as razors, until I hear it—her voice, a door creaking open, then slamming shut, muffled shouting spilling into the corridor. My pulse spikes, wolf teeth gnashing beneath my skin, desperate to hunt, to protect.

The door slams against the wall. My eyes drop to where the scumbag's hands are wrapped around her wrist.

"Let me go, Jett," she snaps, tugging against his grip, voice sharp and defiant.

"Just give me another chance," he pleads, falling to his knees. The corners of her eyes glimmer with unshed tears as he jerks her arm, and something inside me snaps.

I'm on him in a heartbeat, gripping the back of his T-shirt and yanking him upright. My fist clamps down on his wrist with bone-crunching pressure that makes him flinch.

"Let me go!" he yells, struggling against me. "What do you think you're doing? Get your hands off me!"

"You have three seconds to release my girlfriend before I break your wrist," I snarl. "Ten seconds to get out of my sight before I rip you limb from limb."

He deserves it. He hurt her.

"You can't be serious." He scoffs, trying to fight free.

"One," I murmur, forcing patience through the roar in my chest.

You're being too soft on him.

He struggles again.

"Two." I tighten my grip; his face blanches, slick with sweat.

"Fine! Let me go!" He drops Rose and crumples to the ground. He scrambles upright and spits on the pavement. "Good luck. That bitch will ruin your life."

Something primal snaps. My wolf claws at the edges of my control. Instinct takes over. I grab him by the neck and slam him against the building's brick wall.

"What did you call *my mate?*" I growl in his ear, teeth bared, canines elongating, the hot surge of wolf fury pulsing through me like wildfire.

"That *bitch*," he retorts, kicking at the ground, trying to wrench free. "She ruined my chance to showcase my art at the gallery! It would've changed everything for my career!"

"The gallery?" Rose stands tall beside me, voice cold and sharp. "The only reason they even considered you was because of me. After the stunt you pulled on our anniversary, I was done bending over backward for you."

"Bending backward for me?" Jet sneers. "I did everything to get you back—wrote you letters, left you flowers. Hell, I even went down and purchased some dingy love charm, trying to win you back."

"You left that nasty piece of dark magic in her yard?" I snarl, my fists tightening.

"What magic? What is he talking about Carter?" Rose's brows furrow.

"That night I was at your house, I sensed magic that wasn't yours when I checked outside. I got rid of it."

I knew I should've told her when I'd found it, and my suspicions about who had left it, but there hadn't been a good time.

"Oh—so you'll get on your knees for anyone swinging a dick now?" Jett jeers as he jerks against my hold.

"Carter is ten times the man you'll ever be," Rose snaps, fists clenched at her sides, the fire in her eyes daring him to move.

"I'll deal with you later. Let the men handle this." He swings a left hook with reckless force. My head snaps back just in time as his fist grazes my cheek, the sting sharp and hot, a warning.

"Is that all you've got?" I toss my head back, voice low and dangerous. "I've had wolf pups in nappies hit harder than that."

"Why don't you let me down and fight me like a man?" Jett taunts, jerking against my hold, cocky and unafraid.

"A man? I don't think you can handle that." I release my grip on his shirt, and he wobbles unsteadily to his feet.

"That. Bitch. Is. Mine." He lunges at me, eyes wild, rage radiating off him in waves.

"She belongs to no one." I step aside, feeling every muscle in my wolf coil like a spring, and pull my fist back, ready to strike with precision.

Bam.

My fist connects with his nose. Hot, metallic blood sprays across my chest and forearm. The copper tang floods my senses, fueling the wolf surging inside me.

"You broke my nose!" he howls, clutching his face.

"You're lucky that's all he did." Rose's eyes flash.

"You'll regret choosing him over me. I'll show you! Just because everything I did to foul your event opening didn't work—"

"What do you mean..." Rose's hands clench into fists at her sides.

"The decorations? The band having to cancel?" Jett wipes at his dripping nose.

"It was you? This whole time?"

"When that didn't deter you, I thought not having your precious catered macarons would."

"You set the bakery on fire?" Rose gasps, covering her mouth. "You could've hurt someone—or worse."

"All you had to do was take me back."

"You thought by ruining my career I'd come sniveling back to you? That after everything I'd help you get your art into galleries? You're pathetic, Jett. I don't know what I ever saw in you." Rose shakes her head and takes a step back, but Jett lunges for her. She sidesteps and he trips, crashing into the brick wall.

Jett staggers back, howling as he clutches his face. "You fucking bitch."

"Get lost," I growl.

Jett takes one last look at the both of us before bolting around the corner like a coward.

Rose glances up at me, green-blue eyes wide. "Do you think he'll be back?"

"I doubt it," I reply, voice low, muscles still taut. "But if he's stupid enough to... I won't hold back a second time. Some people only learn the hard way." I shrug, trying to rein in the wolf still thrumming in my chest.

Rose lays a gentle hand on my forearm. "Come on. Let's get you inside and cleaned up."

"You're covered in blood," Rose whispers, voice trembling as her fingers lace through mine and pull me toward the narrow bathroom by the office. The scent of her—fresh berries, cream, something wilder—cuts through the metallic tang on my skin.

"I'm fine," I murmur, low and rough. "It's mostly his."

My hand finds her face, cradling it gently; my thumb traces the curve of her cheek as if to prove she's really here. I lift her other hand to my lips and linger against the soft skin on the underside of her wrist. Her pulse flutters beneath my mouth, a frantic, delicate drumbeat that ignites every protective instinct in me.

You went too easy on him. He shouldn't have been able to walk away after that stunt.

"He shouldn't have hit you."

"Hit me? That bastard had no business showing up here, let alone touching you. Tell me you're not hurt." I search her face for the smallest sign of pain, but she shakes her head and slips from my grasp to grab a folded cloth from the shelf.

"No, I'm not hurt. You got there just in time. How did you know?" She meets my gaze, a questioning look in her eyes.

"I just..." I hesitate, searching for words strong enough to hold the truth. "I didn't see you in the crowd, and something in me—something primal—snapped to attention. I couldn't breathe until I found you."

Her gaze softens. "Thank you," she whispers, dabbing the cloth gently along my jaw, the water cool against my heated skin. Thanks to my fast-healing shifter abilities, the bruises and small cuts are nearly gone.

Her breath stills.

"In my world, shifters... we mate for life. We find the other half of our soul and bond. Sometimes it's another shifter. Sometimes—rarely—it's someone from outside our kind." My thumb slides along the line of her jaw, committing every inch to memory. "The moment I saw you, I knew. You're mine. My fated mate. My forever."

"I know," she says simply.

The words hit me like a punch. "You... knew?"

She nods, eyes glistening. "I felt it—that weekend, when I couldn't read your emotions with my magic. I knew you weren't like anyone I'd ever met. I suspected, but I was scared. That's why I ran." She drops her gaze, but I tilt her chin back up, refusing to let her look away.

"Kitten," I murmur, voice rough with feeling, "I will stand at your side for the rest of my life. No matter the miles between us. No matter the dangers. You are mine, and I am yours. Always."

A shy smile tugs at her lips. "I'd like that. And not just because you beat the hell out of my ex." Her gaze locks with mine, steady and sure. "I knew the moment you stepped back into my life."

CHAPTER 23
CARTER

"Come on, Rose, live a little," I tease, lacing my fingers through hers as I tug her across the parking lot.

She digs her heels into the pavement, dress swishing around her thighs. "Absolutely not. You already tricked me into riding that death machine once. I drove here. I'll drive myself home and meet you there."

I glance back at her, smirking beneath the parking lot lights, the silver moon hanging like a spotlight above us. "Your car will be fine overnight, and you'll be more than fine taking the scenic route home with me."

"Carter." She pulls her hand free long enough to gesture at herself. "Look at me. I'm in a dress. I'm not motorcycle-ready."

My grin widens, the wolf rising just beneath my skin at her challenge. Without hesitation, I crouch and tug at the hem of her dress, ripping the seam up to mid-thigh. Goosebumps rise on her legs as cool night air slides across the newly bared skin, pale in the moonlight. I repeat the motion on the other side, ignoring her indignant gasp.

"There," I murmur, eyes locked on hers as the shreds flutter against her legs. "Perfect. Now you're fit to ride my bike."

"Carter!" Her voice is scandalized, but the blush gives her away, a rosy heat even the night can't hide. "It's the middle of the night!"

I cock a brow and step closer until my heat is undeniable. "Exactly. What better time for a ride with your werewolf boyfriend? Or"—I lower my voice, lips brushing the shell of her ear—"are you afraid of the big bad wolf?"

Her sharp inhale is all the permission I need. I sweep her into my arms as we reach the bike, her dress riding higher with the movement. Her laugh catches as I kiss her, hungry and reckless, until we break apart, panting, her lips parted, eyes wide and shimmering.

The backs of her thighs brush the leather seat as I set her down. I drop to one knee between her legs and use my hands to part them. Her breath hitches. My wolf rumbles with satisfaction.

"Or," I whisper, gaze dark and unyielding as moonlight paints her skin silver, "I could just eat my dessert right here."

"Carter, don't you dare!" Her eyes narrow, but she runs her fingers through my hair.

"Why?" I nip at her inner thigh, and her fingers tighten, nails scraping my scalp. My cock throbs, trapped in the confines of my suit. I'm not going to let her win this easily. "Afraid someone will see?"

"Yes," she hisses, but her body says otherwise as her hips buck when my hands slide up the sides of her thighs and over her hips, only thin fabric separating me from her sweet, soft skin.

"Well then, kitten, you have two choices." I stand and lean close to her ear, reaching behind her to unlatch the helmets and hand one to her. "You put this on and brave a moonlit ride with me, or I'll take you right here in the parking lot."

"You wouldn't," she gasps, staring at me.

I smirk, feeling my canines elongate and my wolf stir at the challenge.

"What makes you so certain of that?" I grab her chin and force her to meet my eyes. I run my thumb along her parted bottom lip before claiming her mouth in a bruising kiss.

"You're a beast," she says, roughly taking the helmet from me and sliding it on, then tugging my leather jacket over her shoulders.

"Yes, but I'm your beast."

Just get her home already.

I pull on my helmet and swing my leg over the seat. I live for the moment her arms circle me. Sure enough, she slides on behind me, thighs wrapping around mine, chest firm against my back. Her warmth seeps through my suit like fire, and my pulse spikes at the touch.

The engine roars to life beneath us, vibrating through our bodies. I ease us onto the street, and she clasps her hands tight over my torso. That grip feels like a brand, an anchor, a promise. Gods, I could ride forever like this—just to keep her holding on. I know she doesn't like motorcycles, but her sliding on behind me is more than a physical sign of trust.

"I've got you, kitten. I won't let you fall," I say into the mic, letting go with one hand to find hers and give it a squeeze. I want her to know it's more than reassurance. It's a vow.

Her laugh crackles through the helmet's speakers, but the words are a threat. "I'd haunt you to your last days if you did."

"Is that such a bad thing?" I grin, leaning into a hard turn. She tightens her hold, and my chest swells like it might split from the force of it—her choosing to trust me. Choosing to stay close.

The city blurs behind us as I push harder, hungrier, until the streetlights dissolve into wide stretches of land and trees. Every mile we put between us and the world feels like mine—mine with her. I don't care where we end up, as long as she's here, clinging to me like she belongs.

"This isn't the way to my house," she says, suspicion sharpening her tone.

"Just a little detour. Won't be long." Not long enough, if I'm honest. Never long enough.

The silence that follows isn't empty—it's heavy. Her breath syncs with mine through the mic, her heartbeat thrumming against my back with every bump in the road. I drink in her touch like oxygen, like if she let go, I'd stop breathing altogether.

Finally I turn down a dirt track, ease the bike to a stop, and kill the engine. The sudden quiet hums in my ears, broken only by her soft exhale.

"Come here, little witch." My voice drops to a growl as I twist and tug her onto my lap. She gasps, then locks her legs around my hips, straddling me. My wolf preens. She fits perfectly—carved to sit here, on me. With me. Always.

"Carter..." Her voice trembles, soft and unsure. My name on her lips is my undoing.

I slide my hands up her sides, savoring the feel of her curves until I reach her helmet. I tug it free and let it fall to the grass, then take my own off. Her hair spills around her face, unbound and perfect.

"Look up," I command. She obeys, head tipping back, and the stars scatter like spilled diamonds across the velvet sky. She gasps.

"This is so gorgeous."

"Not as beautiful as you." The words are a whisper, truer than anything I've ever said. My fingers trace the moon charm resting against her chest, right where her heart beats—steady and wild. "I told you I'd see you in the moonlight."

"I thought you said you'd see me in nothing but the moonlight."

Her teasing pulls a low growl from me. My hand slides around her neck, her pulse stuttering beneath my palm. My thumb caresses the fluttering beat while my fingers tighten around the nape of her neck.

"I think my wanton witch likes my little necklace."

"Yes." She leans into my touch, and gods help me, I'd burn the world before I let anyone else hurt her again.

Her breath hitches as I lean in, lips brushing hers. "I'd do anything to keep you here. Anything to stay by your side."

Her tongue flicks across her lips, and I can't hold back. My fingers tangle in her hair, tugging her mouth to mine as my other hand drifts beneath the rip in the hem of her dress. Her heat meets my palm as I stroke through the thin fabric. She gasps, her thighs tightening, her body arching.

"More," she begs. I pull back just enough to see her swollen lips glistening in the moonlight. The sight makes my chest ache with something far more dangerous than lust.

"Soon," I promise, pressing her tight against me, heart to heart. "But not yet. I wanted to bring you away from the noise, the crowd... to remind you that you never have to be afraid with me."

I bury my face in her wild hair, kissing the crown of her head, holding her like I could anchor her to me forever. Because I will. Whatever it takes, however far I have to go—I'll never let her slip away.

CHAPTER 24
ROSE

"How do you feel the event went?" Carter asks, pushing open the front door and guiding me inside, his palm warm at the small of my back.

"Better than I ever expected," I murmur, a lazy smile curling my lips. Magic still thrums through my veins, a low, electric hum from being wrapped in so much energy all night. For the first time in weeks I feel lifted instead of drained; I feel alive.

Before I can say more, Carter pulls me into him, his mouth claiming mine in a kiss that steals the breath from my lungs. Heat floods through me, igniting every nerve as his hands trail down my spine, slow and deliberate, before settling over the curve of my ass, squeezing just enough to make my pulse trip.

"My favorite part," he murmurs against my lips, "was watching you shine while this dress hugged every single curve. You looked like a goddess."

I arch a brow, teasing, "Looked like a goddess?"

He smirks, brushing his mouth over mine again. "A goddess has nothing on my mate." His voice dips lower, rougher, as his teeth graze the edge of my ear. "Soon you'll be wearing nothing but the moon's glow—and my mark on your skin."

The words wrap around me like a promise, and when his lips trail down my neck, heat pools low in my belly, sharp and insistent.

"Does it"—I gasp as my hips press against him, chasing the contact—"leave a mark?"

I'm not afraid, just curious. After I suspected, I scoured the internet in my free time, collecting whatever I could find. Results conflicted depending on the source.

"Not one the human eye can see," he murmurs, breath hot on my skin. "But every shifter, every supernatural worth their power, will know you're mine. Some couples mark it with a tattoo."

"Of the bite mark?" I pull back, raising an eyebrow, fingers reaching up to touch the phantom mark I imagine will soon ghost my skin.

"Sometimes. Or a symbol." His finger traces an outline of the moon on my chest, his touch nearly scalding. "But we don't have to do this tonight."

"I want to." The words rush out of me before I can think—instinct rising like a tide I can't fight.

Ginger winds his orange body around our legs with an impatient meow. Carter chuckles low in his throat, but his eyes never leave mine. "Hey, boy," he says, voice velvety. "Don't worry—we've got a treat for you. But first..." His hand slides to the back of my neck, pulling me in for another kiss that makes my knees go weak.

"Carter," I gasp when he finally pulls back, lips swollen, pulse pounding in my ears.

"Be a good girl," he murmurs, low and commanding. "Go do what you promised me." His palm lingers on my ass before giving it a firm squeeze and a slow, claiming pat. Then he tips his head toward the kitchen, a wicked glint in his eyes. "I'll feed the cat."

I'm still catching my breath when he disappears, but my body hums with the order—thrumming with the knowledge he expects me to obey.

Not five minutes later he fills the doorway. He doesn't just walk in—he owns the space: slacks clinging to his thighs, button-down open at the collar, tie hanging loose, cuffs rolled to reveal the strong lines of his forearms. His gaze pins me like a predator scenting prey.

"That," he says slowly, eyes darkening as they rake down my body, "doesn't look like 'nothing but the moonlight' to me." His tone is a mix of amusement and possession, as if he's already decided exactly what he plans to do.

"It's moonlight-colored," I reply, heat rushing to my cheeks as my fingers smooth the silky cream fabric. It clings to me, whisper-thin, revealing every curve. Even though he's seen me bare, the way he looks at me now makes my pulse stutter and breath catch—like he could strip me without touching a single button.

He steps forward, slow and deliberate, until I feel the heat radiating off him. "Kitten," he murmurs, voice dipping into a growl, "that's not moonlight. That's temptation."

"Oh?" My tongue darts out, wetting my lips.

His fingers skim from my jaw to my collarbone, sending lightning across my skin. "And you," he breathes, leaning down, mouth brushing my ear, "you've been mine from the moment I saw you. Tonight I'm going to make sure you never forget it."

Carter's hands move to his throat, unhurried as he loosens the dark silk tie with a predator's patience.

I rub my thighs together, aching for the friction of his touch—impatient for him to move faster.

"You ready to play, Rose?" His eyes, deep and endless blue, pin me in place, devouring me as if I'm already caught.

The words are low and dangerous, curling through me like smoke. I can barely find my voice.

"Yes," I whisper, pulse thundering in my ears. I want this. I want him. I've wanted—and denied—this man for too long.

"Good girl." His approval drips like honey—rich, commanding, the flash of wolf in his gaze.

How had I ever doubted my feelings for him when a single glance sets my skin on fire?

"Wrists."

My body obeys before my mind can think, hands steady as they slide into his palm. His fingers close over mine with a heat that burns straight to my bones. The silk slips over my skin, sinuous and cool, before he draws it tight enough to make my breath stutter.

I'd never been this vulnerable with anyone—not like this. Especially not with someone whose intent I couldn't read. But I trust Carter.

He grins—wolfish, hungry—and I wonder whether he's more man or beast as he takes the end of the tie between his teeth, yanking so the knot bites just enough to remind me who's in control. My skin hums under the restraint, every nerve alive.

Without a word, he raises my bound wrists above my head, the slow, deliberate lift forcing my body to stretch, my chest to arch for him. The tie whispers against the wood of the bedpost as he fastens it, and I know I'm not going anywhere unless I ask.

"Carter," I gasp, a mix of plea and challenge.

He moves in close, the heat of him pressing along every inch of me. His scent—cedar, leather, and the faintest trace of danger—wraps around my senses. His mouth grazes my cheek, stubble scraping lightly, before his lips hover at my ear.

"You have no idea," he murmurs against my skin, "how beautiful you look like this... mine to feast on. Mine to worship. Mine to mate."

He presses his lips to my skin, tracing a path from collarbone to the soft curve of my abdomen, each kiss claiming me like a brand. My body trembles at his touch, arching instinctively as I tug at my restraints, aching for more.

My pulse hammers in my ears, breath coming in sharp, ragged bursts as his lips linger just a second too long—teasing, tasting, reminding me I'm his. If this is what it feels like now, I don't even want to think about what's coming. I don't want to resist it.

"Carter, please," I whine, body writhing beneath him.

"How attached are you to this?" His smirk is sharp, predatory, as his fingers hook the neckline of my silk nightgown.

"Well—" I start, but he doesn't give me a chance. The fabric rips with a delicious, harsh sound; air floods my skin and I shiver. His mouth claims me instantly—warm, demanding— swirling over one nipple before moving to the other, leaving me breathless. His calloused palms trace down my waist, gripping my hips possessively, digging into flesh as if marking it. Heat curls through me, threatening to overtake everything. I'm burning. I'm his.

His eyes flash dangerously golden as he dips his head between my legs, nuzzling my core.

"Who needs dessert," he murmurs against me, "when I'm craving your sweet center?"

He lifts my ass, and the audacity of the motion makes a whimper escape me. Magic thrums through me, my pulse skyrocketing, heat twisting impossibly tight. My thighs clamp around him without conscious thought, staking claim.

"I want you," I moan as his finger slips inside me, curling with slow, precise mastery. My lips part, a gasp spilling out as waves of pleasure spiral through me.

I've never felt this... not with anyone—except him.

"Patience, kitten," he growls, lips claiming mine while his finger never stops, driving me higher, coiling me tighter. My body shudders, arching against him as the heat explodes, soaking my thighs.

"Why should I be patient when you're taking me over the edge and I can't even return the favor?" I tug at the tie holding my wrists to the bedpost. He smirks—wicked, confident— unbuttons his shirt and peels off his slacks. My eyes track him, hunger coiling low in my belly.

"My little giver," he whispers as he climbs on top of me, the weight of him pressing into every inch of my skin. "You'll have your time. Tonight you deserve to be showered in attention."

When was the last time someone wanted to put me before their own needs?

His free hand drifts toward his pants on the floor, but I tug at my wrists, shaking my head.

"I want to feel you," I whisper, breathless, arching against him in a silent plea. "I'm clean. On birth control. You?"

His eyes darken, molten and raw, as his thumb brushes over my lower lip. "I'm clean. Haven't touched anyone since..."

His voice roughens, breaking just slightly. "Since that weekend we met."

"No one?" I press, needing to hear it again, needing the reassurance written in his gaze.

"No one but you"

He holds my stare, steady and unflinching, and the truth there makes my breath catch.

"I'm going to take you now, kitten." His breath fans my ear, hot and hungry. "And when I finish filling you up, I'm going to mark you as mine." He enters me in one swift, possessive thrust. My cry rips from my throat as he pauses, letting me adjust to the breadth of him, then begins a slow, deliberate rhythm that drives me wild.

I'm his. All of me belongs to him. I've never wanted anything more than this—more than him.

"Not a day has passed when you weren't on my mind," Carter growls, teeth grazing the sensitive skin of my throat as each word rumbles from deep in his chest. "You. Are. Mine." His voice is raw and feral, each syllable punctuated by a thrust that drives him deeper into me. "I love you, Rosemary Sinclaire."

The words hit me like wildfire, igniting every nerve in my body. My hands are still tied, but his growl deepens as he reaches up and releases the silk. My wrists fall free, trembling, and I wrap them around his neck, nails raking the hard muscles of his back. I arch instinctively, feeling the coil of heat in my belly tighten, every inch of me burning for him. I'm his. I've always been his. I can feel it in my bones.

"I love you, Carter Abernathy," I gasp, breathless. "I was a fool for running away. I never want to be apart from you again."

A low, feral growl rumbles through him, vibrating straight

into me. "Fuck... my name sounds like ambrosia on your lips," he hisses, the possessive, predatory edge in his tone making my core clench around him.

He plunges again, harder, faster, and the floodgates inside me open. Pleasure surges like molten lava through every vein. I cry out, hips rolling into him, pressing against every inch of his body. He moans, deep and guttural, the sound vibrating through me as each stroke fills me, swelling until I'm stretched and trembling.

His sharp teeth sink into my neck—pain mingling with lust that sets my senses screaming. I grind against him instinctively, thrusting my hips, nails raking his back, heart hammering, pulse wild. My body quivers, twisting in his arms, riding each wave like a live wire.

He collapses, rolling us onto his back. I straddle him, clinging to the pulse of his heat, his cock buried deep and swollen inside me as my raging need slowly subsides. Strong and possessive hands trace the length of my spine, dragging fire across my skin, pinning me to him, claiming me. I nestle against his chest, listening to the ragged rhythm of his heartbeat.

"Mine," he growls into my hair, voice low and possessive, every syllable vibrating through me.

"Always mine. Forever." I shiver, clinging to him, hips still moving instinctively with each growl and thrust.

I'm his. Only his. Nothing else matters. Nothing ever will.

The world narrows to him—the scent of his skin, the heat of his body, the feral, intoxicating sound of his voice—and I lose myself completely in the primal pull, the raw bond of fated mates.

"How can you ever top a night like tonight?" I ask, lifting a hand to my lips as a yawn escapes.

Carter rolls over and draws me into his side, pressing a kiss to the top of my hair. Our bodies fit together perfectly.

"I plan on spending the rest of our lives trying," he whispers.

I fall asleep curled in his protective embrace, the tingle of magic from his mating mark on my shoulder.

CHAPTER 25
CARTER

ONE MONTH LATER

"**A**re you sure about this?" Rose asks softly, standing in front of the closet with a pile of clothes draped over her arm. She folds each piece with care before lowering it into the cardboard box at her feet. Her voice is steady, but I hear the tremor beneath it—a flicker of uncertainty she's trying hard to hide.

"Am I sure about moving halfway across the country to be with the woman I love?" I can't stop the grin tugging at my lips as I cross the room, sweeping her up by the waist. Her laugh breaks through the heaviness as I spin her in a circle before pressing my mouth to hers in a kiss that leaves no room for doubt. When I pull back, my voice drops to a growl against her lips. "I'd travel the world just to be by my mate's side."

We could show her physically, with more than a kiss, if she doubts our intentions.

Her blush deepens, but when I set her back on her feet her breath comes in shaky bursts. "But... what about the pack?"

My chest tightens at the question. I've never fully let go of the instinct to provide for them, even though letting my brother step into his rightful place as Alpha was what I wanted —what he deserved. I force calm into my voice, steady for her sake. "Connor and Netti have the pack covered. They're ready. And it's not like we'll be gone forever."

I grab the box, tape it shut, and heft it into my arms. "Think about it, Rose. A few weeks to ourselves in a new city? No obligations. Just you and me."

Her lips curve into a reluctant smile, but shadows pool in her eyes. She adds another box to the stack, hands moving almost mechanically. "It won't all be fun and games," she reminds me, tone careful. "We're going there for another job."

"Of course." A chuckle escapes me. "Do you think I could forget the headlines for the Wise Fox Lounge opening? Or the hundreds of calls you got that week?" I glance back over my shoulder as I carry the boxes into the living room. "You're amazing, Rose. People see you. They want what only you can give."

When I turn, she's standing in the doorway, arms wrapped tight around herself. A blush paints her cheeks at my words, but her eyes drop, as if she still doesn't quite believe them.

"What is it, kitten?" I set the box down and close the distance, hooking a finger under her chin to tilt her face up to mine.

She bites her lower lip, worry flickering in her eyes. "I just..." Her fingers toy with the hem of her shirt, twisting it nervously. "Is this what you want? Truly, Carter? To leave your home, the pack—everything—for me?"

You are mine. My mate. My pack.

I brush a stray lock of hair behind her ear, my thumb lingering against her skin. "Is being with you what I want? Rose, it's the *only* thing I've ever been sure of."

"I know you want to be with me. I feel it." She reaches up and touches the place on her neck where the invisible mating mark burns between us. "Since that night, I can feel you with my magic—every emotion, every pull of your heart. It's like... accepting the bond opened something inside me I didn't even know was there."

And goddess, she's right. That bond is alive, thrumming between us like a second heartbeat. I can feel her doubt, her fear, her fragile hope tangled up with mine. I lean in, pressing my forehead to hers, inhaling her scent, grounding myself in the truth only my wolf knows.

She is my mate. My forever. There's no world in which I'd choose anything else.

"Then you—more than anyone—know that when I say I will happily follow you anywhere, I mean it." I press a kiss to her forehead before flicking the tip of her nose. "Plus, I won't shirk my pack duties. I'll be wolf-pup babysitter."

"What—oh, Alexandria!" Rose claps a hand to her forehead. "I'd nearly forgotten I promised her she could intern with me this summer. She's not a pup—she'll be graduating. Are Connor and Netti driving her up, or are we—"

I silence her fretting with a tender kiss. "Don't worry—I've made arrangements for Alexandria to fly out, but not until we're settled and have had some time to ourselves. After the whirlwind of the lounge opening and you finishing up training your replacement at the event hall these last few weeks, I figured some one-on-one time to get to know each other without work or pack obligations would be nice."

"What would I do without you?" Rose smiles, adds one

more box to the stack in the living room, and wipes her hands on her pants. "I think that's the last of it for the movers. Our suitcases are by the door. Ginger is riding with us in the car."

"Everything's taken care of. I already had my important stuff shipped to the new house, and Connor says he'll keep my place ready anytime we want to visit."

"I can't believe we're moving into a house we've never even seen." She runs a hand along the smooth kitchen countertop, and a smile tugs at my lips as I remember the first time I kissed her in this very room. "I'm going to miss this place. This town."

"Rose, you were never meant to settle in one place. Plus, we're just renting, and we've seen photos and videos of the house. It's close to where you'll be working, and there's even a little coffee shop we can walk to." I pull her into my arms, and she melts into my embrace, nuzzling my chest. "You're too good to me. What about you?"

"Well—someone has to be there for any magical mishaps." I grin, and she chuckles, shaking her head.

"I love you, Carter."

"I love you too, kitten." I press a kiss to the top of her head, then scoop up the purring orange ball of fur that had fallen asleep in a warm patch of sunlight filtering through the kitchen window. "It's time for our next adventure."

EPILOGUE

New Years Promises

"This is beautiful," Netti squeals, her breath puffing in the crisp winter air as we climb out of the backseat of our rental car. The sharp bite of pine and wood smoke rushes into my lungs, clean and fresh, as I stretch my legs after what feels like hours winding through snow-laden woods since leaving the airport. The snow crunches under our boots, powdery and untouched, glittering beneath the late-afternoon sun.

"That must be Pinetop," I murmur, pointing down the slope where a cluster of buildings sits like a toy village, smoke curling lazily into the pale sky. The distant sound of a church bell drifts up the mountain on the wind. "It looks so far away now."

"Far enough for peace and quiet, close enough to make a supply run," Connor adds matter-of-factly, though his eyes are glued to the screen of his phone.

"You promised me no work," Netti scolds. She plucks the

phone from his hand and drops it into her purse with a triumphant smirk. "The clan and the business will survive one long weekend without us."

Connor's lips flatten, arms crossing over his broad chest. A puff of steam escapes his mouth in a huff. "I was just doing one final check."

"Sure." Netti rises onto her tiptoes, presses a quick kiss to his cheek, then loops her fingers through his and tugs him toward the cabin. "Hurry up if you want first pick of the bedrooms." She glances back at me with a wink before disappearing inside with her mate.

Their voices fade, leaving only the whisper of wind through branches and creak of trees under their snowy burden. Carter's heat wraps around me from behind, his strong arms banding my middle. His breath fans over my throat, warm and damp in the icy air, before he peppers soft, lingering kisses against my skin. Goosebumps rise beneath his touch, the contrast of his heat and the mountain chill making me shiver.

"You're going to let them win?" I tease, tilting my head toward the door that swallowed Netti and Connor.

In a blink he spins me, pressing me back against the side of the car. Cold metal bites through my sweater, stealing a gasp, while his body pins me—solid, unyielding, hotter than a bonfire.

"I don't need the best bedroom to take my mate." His voice is a rough growl, vibrating low in his chest. His hips press forward, the hard length of him unmistakable against my belly. His teeth graze the sensitive curve of my neck in a sharp nip, a dangerous tease that makes my pulse stutter. "Hell, I don't even need a bed. Don't forget, kitten—I'm a wild animal."

Heat floods low between my thighs, molten, urgent. My

breath catches as every nerve lights up, torn between the mountain air biting at my skin and the feral fire of my wolf pressing into me, branding me as his.

"Carter," I whisper, breathless, before his mouth captures mine.

"Goddess, I love the way my name sounds on your lips. I'll never get used to it." His hand rakes through my hair and I instinctively arch into him.

"If you two don't get inside, you'll freeze to death in the snow," Netti calls, peeking her head out the front door before disappearing again.

"Come on, we should get settled in." I press against his broad chest, but he keeps me pinned. "It's cold out here—and I hear there's a clan of polar bear shifters in these woods.

"Polar bear shifters don't scare me, and I don't share what's mine." His hand slips under my sweater to palm my breast, pinching my nipple as he presses his thigh between my legs. "I can think of a few ways to keep you warm."

I gasp, pressing into his touch as my body betrays me, hips grinding for friction I crave.

"You're such a tease," I pant against his lips as my whole body sparks with pleasure. He swallows the gasp of my orgasm in a kiss before stepping back, a grin plastered across his face.

"That wasn't a tease," Carter growls, heat curling in his words. "That was just the appetizer to what I plan to do with you later." His eyes flick down my body before he turns away with a grin, muscles flexing as he hefts our luggage from the trunk like it weighs nothing.

"Oh, is that so?" My voice comes out lighter than I expect, breath fogging in the cold, but my pulse hammers like a drum. I snatch up my smaller bag and hurry to catch up, boots crunching in the glittering snow as we follow the stone path toward the cabin.

The sharp mountain air burns my lungs, but the moment we step onto the porch I'm greeted by the rich, woodsy scent of pine logs and smoke, the muffled crackle of a fire already burning inside. We stomp the snow from our boots and leave them neatly on the rack by the door before pushing inside.

"Oh," I breathe, words catching in my throat. "This is beautiful."

The cabin feels like something out of a dream. Golden lamplight glows against dark wooden walls. The open floor plan flows seamlessly between kitchen, dining, and living space, everything warm and welcoming. To the left, flames roar inside a stone fireplace, painting the leather couch and low wooden coffee table in a dancing amber glow. Across the way, two rustic doors must lead to the bedrooms, while wide French doors open onto a breathtaking sweep of white snow spilling across ground dotted with towering pines.

"Get comfortable, I'm whipping up a treat," Netti calls from the kitchen, her voice bright.

"You don't have to ask me twice." Carter chuckles. Before I can blink, I'm squealing as he hooks an arm around my waist and hauls me into his lap on the couch. His chest is solid beneath me, warm through my sweater, and the way his arm tightens possessively around my shoulders sends a flush straight to my cheeks.

Connor claims the opposite couch with easy grace, sprawling like a king on his throne—one leg crossed over the other, his arm stretched casually along the cushions. He watches us with a glint of amusement, though he says nothing.

"Do you need any help?" I call toward the kitchen, craning

my neck. Netti answers by sauntering out, apron strings trailing at her waist, pink hair spilling from a messy bun. She sets a tray on the coffee table, the sweet, spiced scent of sugar and chocolate instantly filling the air. Four steaming mugs sit nestled beside a neat pile of cookies dusted with sugar crystals.

"Don't tell me you whipped those up in the five minutes it took us to get inside?" My jaw drops as the peppermint-laced aroma curls around me.

"Five minutes?" Connor snorts, snatching up a mug and inhaling deeply. His sharp eyes cut to us, full of mischief. "I thought I was going to have to send search and rescue after the two of you."

"When did you have time to worry about your brother and his mate when you had your hands all over me?" Netti shoots back, arching one perfectly pink brow at Connor, who smirks into his mug. She turns to me with a softer smile. "No—I baked the cookies ahead of time and tucked them in the luggage. I know Christmas isn't for a couple weeks yet, but with how busy you've been with this new project..." Her gaze flicks between us, warm and knowing. "I figured you could use a little Christmas magic to carry with you on this trip."

"I don't know what I'd do without you." Something swells in my chest at her thoughtfulness: gratitude, affection, and that bittersweet ache that comes from being loved so well. I'd missed them, even though it had only been a few months since we visited the clan to return Dria home after her summer interning with me.

"Well, maybe you could start by being less of a stranger." Netti smiles over the rim of her mug as Connor slips an arm around her and pulls her close. "After all, I'm going to need you to help me plan your best event yet."

"Oh? What would that be?" Curiosity bubbles in my chest.

"My wedding, of course." She beams and holds out her hand; a sizable diamond sits in the middle of an antique white-gold ring. "If you would, of course."

How did I miss that? We've been in the car together for hours.

"There's nowhere else I'd rather be, and no event I'd rather plan." I reach over and squeeze Netti's hand, then lean back, snuggling against my mate. I feel at peace—calm and loved, wanting for nothing.

Carter presses a kiss to the top of my head, and I curl closer into his warmth, the fire crackling behind us, hot chocolate steaming between us, and snow falling silently outside.

Blueberry Scones

2 Cups Flour
3 Tbs Sugar
1 Tbs Baking Powder
1/2 tsp Salt
5 Tbs chilled Unsalted Butter
cut into 1/4 inch cubes
1 Cup Heavy Cream
1/2 to 3/4 cup Dried or Frozen Blueberries
1/4-1/2 cup White Chocolate Chips

Set oven to 450 F.   Line a baking sheet with parchment paper.

Whisk the flour, sugar, baking powder, and salt together in a bowl. Cut in cubbed butter or pulse in food processor until it resembles coarse crumbs. Mix in fruit.

Stir in the cream with a rubber spatula until a dough forms.

Turn dough out onto a light floured counter and knead until it forms a rough, sticky ball (5-15 seconds)

Pat dough into a round circle aprox 8-9 inches wide- cut into 8 wedges and place on an ungreased baking sheet.

Bake until golden brown, about 10-15 minutes. Cool on a wire rack for at least 10 minutes.

MAILING LIST

I truly hope you loved reading Carter and Rose's story as much as I loved writing it.

Be the first to know about my new releases, preorders, and sneak peeks.

Subscribe today to enjoy the spicy companion novelette, Rise of Thorns, to the Thorns universe.

https://fleurdevillainy.myflodesk.com/q8vrseobbq

ALSO BY FLEUR DEVILLAINY

The Vandeleur Trilogy

Sky of Thorns

Secrets of Thorns

Shield of Thorns

To Scorch a Quartz Thorns (novella)

Magickal Morsels

Spellbound Scones

Midnight Macarons

The Cozy Christmas Collective

Cookies & Claws

The Calpa Series

co-written with Johnna Dee

The Clan of Mist

The Clan of Luna

The Clan of Deception (novella)

ABOUT THE AUTHOR

Fleur DeVillainy is an American fantasy author. In the realm of imagination, where love and enchantment intertwine, she crafts tales of extraordinary adventure interwoven with romance, internal growth and found family. By day, she brings healing to little hearts. By night, she lets her pen dance across pages, weaving magical worlds and captivating characters.

When not weaving tales, she finds solace in baking, sewing, and gardening. Join her on the many whimsical journeys through words and discover the wonders that lie within. Check out her series The Vandeleur Trilogy, her comic series Wolf and I, and her co-written Calpa series today!

instagram.com/fleurdevillainy
facebook.com/fleurdevillainy
tiktok.com/@fleurdevillainy

www.ingramcontent.com/pod-product-compliance
Lightning Source LLC
Chambersburg PA
CBHW040331020826
48978CB00013BC/1085